DEAD MAN'S WALK

DEAD MAN'S WALK

Lee Martin

Vaca Mountain Press
Vacaville, California, USA

Vaca Mountain Press
Paperback ISBN 13: 978-1-952380-17-4
Kindle ISBN 13: 978-1-952380-18-1

Library of Congress Catalog Card Number: 89-92628

Interior design by Eddie Vincent, ENC Graphic Services
Cover design by Deirdre Wait for ENC Graphic Services
Cover photograph © Getty Images

Published by Vaca Mountain Press

Visit Lee Martin Westerns on Facebook.

To all of my wonderful family,
and in the fond memory of
my beloved mother,
my beautiful sister Arlene,
our rough riding brothers,
and for Jim Liontas.

DEAD MAN'S WALK

ONE

It was dawn in Salerno. Two rugged men faced each other in the shadowed street. Crumbling adobes hid the people who watched while death awaited a victim. Their silence was filled with fear.

Eli Cole was the taller man, his hawk-like face clean shaven and his thin mouth drawn tight. His lean, hard body was damp with hot sweat, his thin hands were quiet and dry at his sides. His dark hat was pushed back from his brow. The gray double-breasted shirt was open across his broad chest.

Eli's Colt lay waiting at his right hip in a cut- down holster while his big roan pawed the soft earth at a nearby railing.

The stout man facing him was Welchman, soft from easy living, with a sneering smile that refuted fear. The sleeves of his dirty white shirt were pushed up to his thick elbows, and his red beard was wet with whiskey.

Welchman paused, waiting for the first light of the sun to reach Eli's face. Pleasure was hot in the heavy man's chest. This shoot-out would make him a big man in Salerno, the way it used to be when he was flushed with gold. Once more the town

1

would fear and respect him. Women would crawl at his feet. When he killed Eli Cole, he would again be master of them all. Sweat was thick on his face and neck, and his right hand was damp near his holster. His little black eyes were gleaming. His lips were swollen and dry.

In the desert air, dust was catching the first light of the sun as it cleared a nearby roof. Now the glare was on Eli's face. He slowly lifted his left hand to draw his hat down on his brow.

At that moment the two men could hear the town as if it had drawn a deep breath in its silence. They felt the anxious gaze of the onlookers, held by the fascination of impending death.

As Eli lowered his left hand from his hat brim, Welchman drew. Eli's right hand whipped his gun from its holster.

Both men fired, their shots crackling the stillness and then echoing along the street. Neither man seemed to move. Their shadows remained long and narrow up the dusty pathway between the adobe walls of the town.

Perfume, thick and unpleasant, filled the air. A woman was standing in the street near Welchman, a shawl about her shoulders, trembling hands clasped to her breast. Long, dark hair draped her thin, painted face. There were no tears in her eyes. Only agony and pain.

As Welchman dropped to his knees, she ran to him, knelt, and cradled his face against her. His big body trembled as blood came to his mouth. His eyes were glassy by the time Eli Cole came over to look down at him.

The woman hugged Welchman, and hatred filled her eyes as Eli knelt and shook the dying man's arm.

"Where's Cassidy?" Eli demanded.

Welchman couldn't see him, not anymore, and the big man slumped against the woman, lifeless. Unable to hold him, she let his body slide to the ground.

Eli stood up, holstering his gun, his face lined with exhaustion. Ignoring the fury in the woman's eyes, he turned away.

People began to appear from doorways, and Eli walked to his big roan stallion where it waited impatiently down the street. People watched with awe. They had seen death at the firing of a gun, a Colt so fast that it could leap into his hand almost before he touched it.

The woman's shrill voice knifed the stillness behind him: "Yellow Creek! There you'll find him, and there you'll die!"

Eli took the reins, checked the cinch, and swung into the saddle. He looked at the woman where she stood with her shawl falling from a shoulder.

Eli Cole turned his roan away and rode slowly out of town, heading northward toward the distant mountains and the mining camp known as Yellow Creek, one of the new strikes in Arizona Territory.

It was the fall of 1876 in a wild, unsettled land, and Apaches were a constant danger. General Custer and his troops had just been destroyed by the Sioux up north. It was a hazard just to be in the saddle.

Eli Cole had known the bitterness of the Civil War's last year. Wearing the blue coat of a Union captain, he had led men and led them well. He had been a weary but proud man, eager to return to ranching. But now, at thirty-five, he could look back only on ten years of hunting men.

The sun became hot on the desert trail. Insects rose from the blue sage as he passed. Overhead, a black buzzard circled in the hazy sky and observed the lone rider.

The smell of Eli's sweat mingled with that of his mount. He pushed back his hat to cool his brow, a brow with lines too deep and harsh for a man his age. His black hair was damp, and perspiration dripped down his sideburns.

As his stallion bucked at the scratching brush, he reached down to stroke its powerful neck.

"Easy, old fella. We've a piece to go."

In two days he would reach Yellow Creek, where he would kill another man, the last of seven who had murdered his family during a wild race from a posse some ten years back. They had changed their names, living high on their stolen gold, but he had found them one by one. Four others had made it their fight. They were all dead but the leader, Tom Cassidy, the most dangerous of them all.

At his camp that night, Eli sat down by the flickering fire in the chill of a desert gully and then took out the reward poster. Using a charred stick, he crossed off another name. Only Cassidy was left, a man without a face or description. He folded the paper and shoved it back inside his shirt. As he stared into the fire, their faces continued to haunt him. Their voices still rang in his ears.

"Blast you!" the first had shouted. Others had been more profane in their last breath.

Eli shut out their faces with a hatred that, over the years, had become fired with a hunger to finish the hunt.

In the hot coals he could see the charred ruins of his ranch house. He had just been mustered out of the Army. He had ridden home to his new wife and his parents. But they were no longer there. The story had been harsh, told from the lips of his dying father, who had crawled into the arms of the posse. His tale of horror had been reported to Eli.

"The Cassidy bunch," the sheriff had said. "Seven of them."

When the faces of those he killed would appear in his campfire, he would cover them with the sight of three graves. He would remember that Cassidy had beaten his beautiful bride and let her burn to death. He would not rest until they were all dead.

As Eli lay in his bedroll and listened to the far- off call of a lone coyote, he stared at the distant stars in the black sky. He was now a gunfighter, a name, a reputation, someone feared and someone to kill. But he was not proud of what he had become. Perhaps it was fitting that he and Cassidy should die together in Yellow Creek, high in the mountains, with no one to mourn them.

He slept without rest, fighting wild, senseless dreams.

In the morning he awakened in a sweat, gun in hand. He sat up in his blankets and listened to the silence. Climbing out of the gully, he looked at the empty land around him. Only his grazing roan shared his world.

Suddenly he felt spooked and unbearably alone. As quickly as possible, he broke camp and saddled his roan, already snorting at something in the creosote. "Easy, old fella," he said as he mounted, mostly to hear his own voice.

Eli tried to pull himself together, but the desert never seemed to pass. The mountains ever remained on the far horizon, a blue shadow beyond the rolling sage and sand. The sun was close, unbearable to anyone but a man in a hurry.

He tried to concentrate on the Apache danger. He knew they would cover themselves with dirt and lie in wait. A man never knew they were there until it was too late. They were fierce, angry, fearless fighters. Eli felt a kinship with them. He had not known fear for ten years.

Overhead, three buzzards appeared and circled slowly.

"Not yet, you stinkin' polecats," he said aloud.

By the end of the day, the Wolfpack Mountains began to rise in the northern sky. Eli camped at last in the foothills, where the air was cool and thin. The night was cold. Stunted, weathered junipers rose among the rocks.

In the morning he rode on, his roan unhindered by the thin air and mountains as they climbed. Sage and juniper covered the rolling foothills. Higher, ever higher, he rode. The trail was marked with deep wagon ruts, an occasional grave, and hoof-prints burned into the earth by time and sun. A straggly rope dangled from the limb of a barren tree.

In the cool shadows of evening, with the sun's last light on the rim of the hills, he reined up. At the foot of the black ridges beyond, he could see the lights of Yellow Creek, flickering and ghostly. The town was nestled against the first rise. Beyond it to the north were the snow-covered mountains where he had once trapped with his father.

As his roan fought the bit, the saddle creaked beneath Eli with a new loudness. He was conscious of his own breathing, of his sweat and dried face, his trembling hands. His mouth was burning dry, and his body ached from the hard ride that had brought him to this grassy spot.

It would be another waiting game. Cassidy could be a respected citizen or the town drunk, but sooner or later, he would show his hand. Eli would have to speak of what he sought and let them know his name. He had to force Cassidy into the open and a fair fight. He thought of the sheriff who had found his father.

"You be mighty careful," the man had told him. "Cassidy ain't no ordinary man. He'd as soon gut you as look at you. He shot a man in the back down near Tucson."

Eli started the roan down the rocky, dusty trail to a dry creek bed, and then followed it in the light of a half-moon. His right hand rested on his gun, feeling its coldness. Ten men had already died under the fire of his Colt.

He circled until he could enter the single street from the east. Here on the left side were the saloons, with laughter and music coming from their swinging doors. Across from these buildings, on open ground, were camps and tents with flickering fires. Amid a smell of meat and gravy, a baby's cry rose above mumbling voices.

Moonlight revealed some of the mines dotting the ridge behind him and to the north. Eli followed the street toward the respectable part of town, separated by a wooden bridge over a dry creek.

He felt the difference the minute he was over the rattling structure. On the right was the long, rambling general store, housing the assay office and express office. A stage arrival was crossed out on the blackboard by the window. Next to it was a notice that Colorado was now a state. A black horse was asleep in harness at a buckboard in front of the store. Lights were dim inside.

The street seemed deserted otherwise. Next to the store was a barber shop. As he continued west, he came to an open clearing, also on the right. At the rear, an adobe icehouse arose out of the earth. In the center of the clearing stood a tall, naked jail tree, its leaves long dead. Chains from the trunk led to neckbands, empty in the dust, gleaming ever so slightly in the moonlight.

"Shoot me," a man in such a neckband had once pleaded with Eli. It had been at a dirty border town, a terrible sight he could never forget.

A broken, abandoned wagon lay in a heap at the far edge of the clearing, near the next building, which was the Town House, evidently a respectable saloon. A sign announced tables for ladies. A piano was playing "Red River Valley." Eli could see three men at a table near the swinging doors. They were engrossed in a card game, with smoke drifting up from their twisted cigarettes.

The Sims Hotel was next, a rambling, rather elegant white structure with a grand entrance. There was a large balcony with fancy iron railing. He thought he saw a woman up there, watching him, but she was just a shadow. He turned his roan about and rode back down the other side of the street.

There was the Sims Banking and Express House, followed among other buildings by Sims Mining Supplies. He would have to learn why the man was so wealthy, but tomorrow would be soon enough.

He continued on to the livery that was set back from the street, across from the general store. An old man, stooped and gnarled, came out of the entrance to the huge barn.

"Fine animal, mister. You can leave 'im with me.

"Like to bunk here myself," Eli said.

Watching Eli enter the livery, the woman on the hotel balcony gripped the iron rail with a slim white hand. A slight breeze lifted her long yellow hair from her shoulders. She drew a white shawl more closely about her, but the chill of the evening was no colder than the chill in her green eyes. A pained smile on her lips brought a crease to the long white scar on her left cheek. The thin scar marred what was truly a beautiful face.

Her name was Eve Bennett, and for a moment she had mistaken Eli for her fiance, Will Gunnison. She had been awaiting him for weeks, and praying he would never arrive.

Back in her room, she sat on the bed, turned up the lamp, and then lay back to stare at a cobweb on the ceiling. Rather than see her father hanged for murder in St. Louis, she had agreed to journey west to marry the only alleged witness, Will Gunnison.

Her father's sobbing confession that the charges were true had left her shattered. He had sworn, however, that it had been self-defense. Will Gunnison and two of his friends were ready to swear otherwise unless she married him.

Once she had consented to marry Will, he had become warm with affection and promise.

"You'll always have everything you want," Will had said. "You want the moon? It's yours."

Despite his rough ways, he had tried to bring romance and excitement to their trip west. He had been a perfect gentleman, to her surprise. He had bought her an expensive wardrobe and jewelry, but he had not taken advantage of her. Then he had left her during the journey, promising to meet her in this place.

She felt old at twenty-one, lonely and tired, living a nightmare. The satin softness of her green dress no longer felt smooth and tingly. The glittering ring on her finger was heavy. The feather mattress was soft and luxurious, but it wasn't home.

A tear slid across her scarred cheek into her soft yellow hair.

*　*　*

9

Eli was awakened before dawn by the cold nose of his roan. He sat up, gun in hand.

"What is it, old fella?" he asked.

The roan snorted and tossed its head.

"Yeah," Eli said. "It's a bit stuffy in here."

He tied up his bedroll in the light of the lamp burning near the door. The livery was full of horses. An old drunk was asleep near the back wall. Upstairs in the loft, several out-of-luck drifters were spread out and snoring.

Stiff and weary, his face bristly and his body dirty, Eli decided it was time to see the barber. He fed his horse and walked to the door of the livery. The sun was barely above the northern ridge where the mines were bustling with activity. Each hole looked like a hornet's hollow, oozing dust and discard in long, downward trails. Junipers and brush were the major vegetation, but he knew that farther north were the pines and snowline. He was beginning to hunger for that clean, breathless land.

The street was empty, and so was the barber shop. The sleepy barber offered him a shave and bath for fifty cents.

"You plannin' to get your own diggin's?" the barber asked.

Eli leaned back in the chair, his hand on his Colt, and the barber became a little nervous.

"Lots of gold up there," the barber said. " 'Course, some men have other ways of makin' a living."

Realizing that he might put his foot in his mouth, the barber became silent. He worked carefully on Eli's beard and cropped hair.

"Know a man named Tom Cassidy?" Eli asked.

"Wasn't he some outlaw a few years back?"

"Does he live around here?"

"No one here by that name, but then I reckon a lot of folks here are walkin' around with names they wasn't born with."

After a hot bath, Eli still felt the grime of his clothes, and he set out along the creaking boardwalk to the general store. People were bustling about, anxious to do their business before the heat of the day. No one paid him any heed as he entered the store.

He bought a double-breasted gray shirt and Levi's, and he changed in the back room while an elderly lady argued with the bald storekeeper over the price of some linen.

Wearing the same black hat with the wide brim but feeling cleaner in new clothes, Eli strapped on his Colt, paid the storekeeper, and left.

Wagons were moving about. Youngsters were playing in the street between the horses and dogs. He saw the swarthy giant of a smithy near the livery, bending over a horse's hoof. The smell of hot coals, leather, and hoof scrapings drifted from the shed.

The scent of breakfast from the Town House drew Eli off the street and inside. A man at a nearby table was eating steak and eggs. In the rear, a group of men were arguing. The bartender, sleeves rolled up and wearing a fancy green vest, pulled at his handlebar mustache and then, with a sour face, continued to wipe his glassware.

Eli found a corner table near a window and sat down with his back to the wall. The place didn't smell of smoke and tobacco like most saloons. There were curtains, and fancy lamps, and a huge glass chandelier. There were no drunks asleep at the table. Proper ladies entered freely, and two of them chattered at a far table while being served coffee.

Above the bar, a painting of a woman, draped respectfully

with a velvet negligee, seemed to have had the gown painted over her previous exposure.

The waiter was young and clean and cheerful, and he brought Eli his coffee, steak, and eggs. When he returned to collect payment after Eli had finished his meal, he was startled by Eli's question:

"I'm looking for a friend—Tom Cassidy. Know him?"

"Not this side o' town. Can't say about the other."

Eli paid him and finished his coffee. It was black and thick, good to swallow, hot in his dry throat. Word would now spread. Cassidy would know that someone was on his trail. If he had heard about his dead cohorts, he would know it was Eli Cole.

Eli looked at the men in the back of the room. Bearded and dusty, they paid him little heed. The young waiter stopped and talked with them, but they shook their heads. No one would know who Cassidy was, except Cassidy himself.

Eli set down his cup and went out into the warm sun, soon moving into the shade. A small boy of about five came running around the corner with a stick gun, followed by another and another. A fourth came to chase them, his stick gun a rifle, and he stumbled into Eli.

"Sorry, mister," the boy said breathlessly, his face round and red. "We gotta get that killer."

"Killer?"

"We're the posse and he's Eli Cole."

The boy skirted Eli and followed the other boys into the alley behind the hotel. His remark left an invisible knife in Eli's gut.

A fat man was sitting on a bench in the shade. After wiping his face from the heat, he looked up at Eli and nodded.

"Hot, ain't it, mister?"

"Soon will be. I'm lookin' for a friend. Tom Cassidy."

"Not this side of town, and I ain't heard the name on the other."

"I notice there's a mighty enterprising man here," Eli said. "The name of Sims is on everything I see."

"Yep, he about started things around here. While most were up diggin' holes, he was settin' up here to take it away from them. He might know your friend."

"Where would I find this Sims?"

"Might try the bank across the street. He likes to count his money."

Eli dodged a wagon loaded with buffalo hides and stench, driven by a man who looked like a buffalo himself.

Inside the fine bank with its red carpet and grand windows, he ignored the guard who was half asleep and bored. Two elderly women in finery were chattering at the teller's window. The teller, framed by iron bars, was pretending to enjoy the conversation.

In the south corner of the bank, behind a huge walnut desk, sat a huge man. His face was puffed with fat. He was clean shaven, with rolls of skin at his neck, and nearly bald. As he watched Eli approach, his little gray eyes moved from Eli's six-gun to his stern face.

Fingering the vest of his dark pin-striped suit, the banker smiled. On his desk a gold sign announced, *Reginald Sims, President.* Here was a man not content to hide his success in a back office. He wanted to be out front, to watch the money walk in, and make sure it didn't walk back out.

Eli paused and studied the man for a moment. Surely, even

after ten years, this couldn't be Tom Cassidy, a mean, surly outlaw who had ridden hard and fast and killed ruthlessly.

"Good morning, sir," Sims said. "Please sit down."

Eli nodded, sat down in the wooden chair, and refused a cigar. Sims put his fingers together and smiled.

"Now then, sir, what can I do for you?"

"I'm looking for a man. Tom Cassidy."

"Don't know the name. You a lawman?"

"Not likely."

"Then maybe you're on the wrong side of town."

The banker's smile was calculated to keep himself from being shot, but there was sweat on his nose.

"Thank you for your time," Eli said, about to rise.

"No offense intended, mister. The only law here is a miners' court when needed. Every few months the U.S. marshal passes through. Most people here—well, we sort of mind our own business."

Eli no longer heard the banker. He was gazing at a young woman who had entered the bank. She was gliding across the shiny wooden floor in a green satin dress that swished as she moved. Her proud body was so erect and graceful that the thin white scar was meaningless on her incredibly beautiful face.

Her yellow hair was full and glistening and flowing on her shoulders, not set in tight curls as was the fashion. Never had Eli seen such a lovely woman. Her features were delicate, her lips full but trim, her eyes large and shining like emeralds in a face the soft color of peaches.

Eli could not take his gaze from her. For the first time in many years he felt a tug in his chest, the reaction of a man to the woman who could mean something to him.

"Eve Bennett," Sims said, moistening his thick lips. "She was to meet her fiance in Yellow Creek, but he hasn't showed."

A worried, thin-faced cashier scurried over to them. He bent close to the banker, his voice low.

"Miss Bennett wants another loan."

"Well, give it to her," Sims said. "Give her anything she wants."

The cashier hurried back to his window where the woman stood with her back to the banker and Eli, perhaps too embarrassed to thank the fat man behind the desk.

"I've seen a lot of women," Sims said quietly, "but I never saw one like her. Just thinkin' about her makes a man crazy in the head."

As Eli started to rise, Sims held up his hand.

"Wait, please. What did you say your name was?"

"Eli Cole."

Sims's eyes grew round, and he couldn't speak.

Eli stood up, having seen that look before.

Sims said, "I've heard of you. You're the fellow who hunts men down. Some sort of vendetta. I hear you're fast, maybe the fastest there is. I have to talk to you. Please sit down."

Reluctantly, Eli slid back into the wooden chair. He turned just in time to see Eve Bennett walking toward the door. She moved as if she were walking on velvet, her every step one of beauty and grace.

"I could sure use a man like you," Sims said.

"I don't hire out."

"There have been holdups and killings on both sides of town. As mayor, I've tried appointin' our own law, but they were always gunned down. Look, I won't hedge with you. We need law and order or my own investments aren't worth a hoot. If you were sheriff, maybe we'd have a chance."

"I'm not a lawman."

"Just think about it, Mr. Cole. It'd be a job while you're lookin' for this Tom Cassidy fellow. If you was to tin' a badge, ain't no one either side of this town would walk on the wrong side of the street. Will you at least think about it?"

While Eli considered the job offer, his thoughts were also on Eve Bennett. A beautiful woman, a respectable job, for Eli Cole?

He shrugged, knowing he should never think about the impossible. He saw his reflection in the window and stared at it—that tall, lean, hard man with the hawk-like face and thin mouth, the furrowed brow, that man with the low-cut holster. No, it wasn't possible. And yet…

"Listen, as mayor I have the power to appoint you till we can get up an election. Believe me, your name would calm things down around here. Do you know we've had three bank holdups in the last year? Not to mention the loss of a few gold shipments."

"I'll think on it."

"I'd make sure you'd want for nothin'."

Eli stood up just as another young woman entered the bank. She was wearing rich brocade and blue silk, with her brown hair in big curls under a wide, feathered bonnet. Her smile was pretty under the flashing blue eyes. She had a slightly turned-up nose and a lot of self-confidence, probably from finishing school.

"Mr. Cole," Sims said, "my daughter, Doris."

Eli tipped his hat and turned away, leaving them to stare after him as he left the bank. Doris watched him pass out of sight, and she folded her arms with pleasure. Then she sat down to smile at her frowning father.

"Well," she said, "there goes a real man."

"He's a gunfighter, a killer. This is no man to play your little games with."

"Oh, Daddy, he's the first real man to hit town."

"I offered to make him sheriff, but I don't think he'll take it."

"Maybe I can help, Daddy. Invite him for supper. I'll charm him."

"I didn't tell him the last sheriff was shot in the back, just like the last deputy marshal."

"He wouldn't be afraid."

"I never saw a man who was less afraid. He's Eli Cole."

She brightened. "Eli Cole? The one they call The Hunter?"

"That's him."

"They say he's killed a dozen men and that he's the fastest gun alive."

"Let's hope he is. If he becomes sheriff, he'd better live up to his reputation."

"He's not like any man I've ever met. Why, all the women in town will envy me for knowing him."

"And suppose you get interested in him and he kills your old man instead?"

"Oh, Daddy, don't be silly. Now I'm going to pick up my new dresses. Don't forget to pay the bill."

"I should have bought that store when I had the chance," he muttered.

Rising with a swoop, she walked around to kiss him on the head. She hurried to the door, stepping out into the sunlight, looking for signs of Eli Cole.

Disappointed, she pouted as she crossed to the general store. All she could think about was that tall, lean, dark gunman, his indifference and coldness. Her father could play all the games he wanted. She had a game of her own to play, and she very seldom lost.

TWO

*T*wo days had passed. The town was whispering about Eli Cole, who was there "hunting someone named Tom Cassidy." They had heard about Sims's offer to appoint Cole sheriff. It was known that he had not as yet answered the call.

People crossed the street to avoid walking near Eli. He was an ominous figure, tall and lean and sharp of face, his gleaming eyes dark and haunted. He walked like a hunter on a trail of vengeance.

Doris was waiting, eager for him to call on her. She wanted him to come to supper, to sit in her parlor and succumb to her games, her coy tricks, her charms.

At the other end of town, gunfire was often heard. The black ridge, riddled with mines, was also riddled with bullets. There was a rumor that a dance-hall girl had been strangled in the east side of town. Two men were buried in two days, also on the east side of town.

Many times every day, Eve Bennett would appear on the balcony of the hotel. Sometimes she would stroke the scar on her left cheek, as if to remind herself it was there. Then she would disappear like a mirage, taking her meals in her room.

On that hot afternoon, Eli sat in the shade on a bench next to the Town House. He watched a wagon leaving the general store. A few horses were at the hitching rails, their tails switching away the flies.

Farther along the street a dog lay panting in the shade, but otherwise the street was empty. Piano music drifted from inside the Town House. A few voices were raised in anger at a poker table near the door.

"Noisy in there," the barber said, pausing in the shade.

"Reckon so."

"Heat gets to everybody."

Eli nodded, and the man went inside.

Wiping the sweat from his face, Eli tried to picture Tom Cassidy. In ten years the man could have changed his appearance. He could still be wealthy with the gold, or he could have thrown it away on whiskey and women. There was nothing more than a vague description from the old sheriff at the time. Average height and nondescript face. It could fit any man.

The only thing Eli could count on was the name of Eli Cole. They had all known he was hunting them. That was all he had ever needed to flush them out.

He considered the men he had met here. There was Sims, fat on all his money. It could be money he had made from the miners, but it could also be stolen gold, hoarded and invested. There were other men here just as wealthy, on both sides of town.

Shifting his weight on the bench, Eli took out his knife and began to whittle on a chunk of wood. He watched a rider approaching from the east.

The man was letting his sorrel pick its surefoot way up the

dusty street. There was a bedroll behind his cantle. On his black vest, a badge caught the sunlight. His brown hat shaded most of his square face, but he was gray at the temples. Slight of build and medium in height, around fifty, he looked weary and somber, exhausted from the heat.

The lawman reined near the livery and dismounted. A boy of about ten, freckled and in ragged Levi's, came hurrying up to him. The weary traveler allowed him to take his horse's reins. They talked a moment. Then the lawman removed his bedroll. The boy led the horse into the livery.

After a long glance at the jail tree and empty chains, with never a look toward Eli, the lawman walked over to the Town House with the bedroll over his shoulder. Even as he neared the shade, the lawman appeared not to notice him.

Eli sat quietly as the stranger entered the saloon. The pale blue eyes had not set directly on Eli, but he had felt them.

Knowing that a lawman was the best source of information, Eli slowly pocketed his knife, stood up and stretched, and then entered the saloon. The traveler had passed through the almost empty room and bypassed two men at the bar. He chose to stand alone at the far end. He poured his own drink, his back to the wall. The two saloon women, dressed more properly for this side of town, stayed away from him.

Eli walked across the room, conscious of his heels thumping the floor. He moved to within a few feet of the lawman, but didn't look at him. He disliked the taste of whiskey, so he ignored the barkeep.

The room was silent, for they were being watched. Yet from where they stood at the far end, their conversation could not be easily heard. The man didn't look up as Eli spoke.

"You the Federal marshal?"

"That's right. Marshal Kline."

"I'm looking for a man. Tom Cassidy. Know him?"

"I know of him, from years back. You a bounty hunter?"

"No."

"Friend of his?"

"No."

The lawman considered this. As if uninterested, he looked from his glass to the painting of the woman above the bar. The woman's gaze was beseeching, her smile soft.

"Why is it that a woman always wants?" Kline muttered.

Eli shrugged, and still they did not look at each other. Kline continued, sounding angry at the world, particularly the women in it:

"When they're born, they cry the loudest. The bigger they get, the more they want. When they finally hook some poor fool, they want a cook and a maid. They want him to quit smokin' and quit drinkin'. They want him to do this and do that." "You married?" Eli asked.

"I'd rather wrestle a porcupine."

Eli almost grinned. It cracked and hurt his tough face, for it had been many years since he had felt like smiling. He liked this grizzled man and wasn't sure why. He saw their reflections in the mirror, gunfighter and lawman, side by side.

The marshal kept gazing up at the painting. Somber and angry, he downed another drink before continuing.

"Women can also be young and helpless, like the girl I just buried. Had to leave a letter for her folks, who had left her there alone at a ranch house. A child, and no trace of the ones that done it. Wasn't Apaches, either."

The man's blue eyes nearly closed, as if he were fighting tears he felt and could not shed. "A child," he added. "Not even a woman."

Kline downed another drink, but it wasn't helping him. Eli could see that the man was fed up with his job. This was a hard man who felt pain and couldn't show it or accept it.

Eli began to think of the posse, of the sheriff into whose arms his father had crawled, burning from the fire where two women had already died. That sheriff must have cried that night, sometime when he was alone in the dark. The way Kline would later tonight, when none could see.

Eli realized something as he stood next to the lawman: Though he had killed ten men, he could still feel for another human being. And he could see beyond his own grief.

Both men stood wrapped in their thoughts. Suddenly, Kline turned to gaze at Eli, and his blue eyes darkened. For the first time the two men were directly studying each other. Then Kline looked past Eli, through the swinging doors, and across to the bank where Sims was stepping into the sunlight.

"Here he comes," Kline said. "First thing he'll say is, 'Marshal, I thought you'd never get here!' And second thing he'll say is, 'Doris has been asking about you.' Now there's a woman who really wants."

Eli felt his face cracking into a half smile. They watched the fat banker puff his way over to the saloon. All smiles as he hurried inside, Sims waved to them. In his shirtsleeves, short of breath, he made it to the counter next to Eli. His round eyes seemed ready to pop out of his face as he spoke.

"Marshal, I thought you'd never get here! The stage was held up again last week. The guard was shot. You've got to appoint another deputy marshal. It's been a year since we had any law in town."

Kline nodded. "Hello, Mr. Sims."

The banker caught his breath. "Doris has been asking about you, Marshal. I know she'll insist you come to supper tonight."

"I'm dirty and I stink," Kline said.

"But you've no prisoner," Sims persisted, "and I'll bet you were plannin' on a bath and shave anyhow."

"I was," Kline said. "Tell me, have you seen the Conners family?"

"Sure did. Yesterday they was in, borrowing money for a new crop and takin' candy back for their youngster. Left last night, I reckon."

Kline's face was grim and even darker now. There would be no one to eat the candy.

"What about supper?" Sims insisted.

Kline shrugged. "All right."

"Eight o'clock, then," Sims said. "And Doris will insist you come also, Mr. Cole."

Eli nodded, and Sims hustled away. Eli felt his face growing hot with his name hanging in the air. He felt the lawman's gaze burning his profile. There was a long moment of silence before the man spoke. Eli didn't turn.

"What's your given name, Mr. Cole?"

"Eli."

Kline seemed to taste the name on his lips before he spoke again. "Eli Cole. Every year you seem to take out another notch. Last week it was Salerno, right?"

Eli stared at his hand on the bar. "Yes."

"Heard it was a fair fight. Heard they all were. Also hear tell you're pretty fast. And I heard what happened to your family. Is Tom Cassidy next?"

"He's the last. His trail stops here."

"And you use yourself as bait."

"It's worked before. Do you know what Cassidy looks like?"

"Afraid not."

Eli gripped the edge of the bar, trying to break it.

"Look, son," the marshal said, "taking the law in your own hands can leave you dead. You've been lucky till now. I hear tell Cassidy is the meanest of the bunch and worth five thousand dollars."

"I've never collected on the rewards."

"I know."

"You riding my trail?"

Kline tossed coins on the bar and picked up his gear. He turned to Eli. "I'll be at the hotel. Meet me there. You can let me know after supper."

"About what?"

"About totin' a badge for me. What else?" Kline turned and walked out, leaving Eli staring after him. The hum of the people in the saloon seemed loud suddenly. Eli slowly made his way outside, where he could see the lawman walking toward the hotel. He felt fingers clawing at his insides as he sat down in the shade.

Eli Cole wearing a badge? Not a sheriff's badge for Sims and his merchants but the badge of a U.S. deputy marshal? Unbelievable. Other gunfighters had taken up a badge, but Eli Cole was no gun- fighter for hire. He was a rancher who had been on a manhunt. He didn't want to live by the gun. He wanted the killing to be over and finished. Kline had shaken him with the offer, and Eli liked the man, making it tougher to say no.

The sun was hotter now, and Eli walked to the hotel. He passed through the lobby to the pink and white dining room where the tables were all empty. Sitting in a corner, he ordered pie and coffee from a man in a white apron, a man whose face he didn't see. All he could think of was Kline and maybe heading for Oregon when this was over.

He became conscious of someone standing at his side, of someone scented with violets. He looked up into the wondrous face of Eve Bennett. He stood up awkwardly, unable to stop staring at her. She was wearing blue and looked like the fairy queen in a picture book he had once read.

Her green eyes glistened. Glorious blond hair was swept back from her face in long, flowing waves. It was more than her delicate features that made her so beautiful. There was a haunted depth about her. She made a man want to stand between her and whatever was threatening her, to fight for her, and, yes, to hold her. It was a feeling a man needed, and Eli was grateful that it was coming back to him.

"May I join you?" she asked.

They sat down together, and the waiter returned.

She ordered coffee in that soft, musical voice. Once she received the steaming cup, she turned to Eli.

"I'm Eve Bennett."

"Eli Cole."

"Is it true that you always face a man in a fair fight?"

"Yes."

"And you've always been too fast for them?"

The scar on her left cheek was silver against her peach-colored skin. She lifted the cup and saucer. They rattled and she set them back down. Quiet for a moment, she stared at her hands, and then she spoke as she stood up.

"I'm sorry," she said. "It was a bad idea."

Eli rose to her side. "Are you in trouble?"

Slowly, they sat back in their chairs.

"I'll be all right," she said.

"I don't hire out, but if I can help in any other way, let me know."

"It's just that when I saw you, I thought you were the answer. Now I realize that I could never go through with it. I'm sorry I bothered you, Mr. Cole."

"You must be hurtin' mighty bad."

She nodded sadly and rose from her chair. Eli stood also. It was obvious that she was still shaken from what she had voiced earlier.

"Good day, Mr. Cole," she said softly, then moved away.

Eli stared after her, wanting to follow, all the while knowing he couldn't. The more painful thing, he realized, was the knowledge that he was not a dead man, not anymore. It hurt to be alive. It had been better when he was numb with hatred. To feel, to ache, to want, was to be more vulnerable.

And for the first time in ten years his hands were damp. As he walked to the bar to lean on it, he found himself shaking. He had heard that the woman was going to marry a Will Gunnison, who had to be an evil man to make her so distraught. It was a dangerous feeling to want to hate a man he hadn't met, especially when it was because of a woman.

That night, ambling along the boardwalk, he saw Kline waiting by the hotel. Together they walked toward a big white house at the edge of town. Kline knocked on the solid oak door. Waiting, they glanced back down the dark street. Window lights traced the dust in the air. Far away, a coyote's howl lingered.

The door opened and then Sims greeted them in his smoking jacket of fine brocade. Beaming, he led them into the parlor and pointed to the wealth of crystal dangling above.

"That chandelier came all the way from St. Louis," the fat man said. "Worth a fortune."

Doris came into the room. She was wearing yellow satin, and she waved her hand at the rosewood piano.

"Relax, gentlemen, we have a cook. But I do play the piano, so you can worry about that."

"Came from St. Louis too," Sims said proudly.

Money, Eli thought. That was what it took for finishing schools and a fine piano or crystal chandelier. He studied Sims and wondered again if his wealth came from stolen gold. As Doris left, the men took drinks at the walnut bar in the corner.

Sims lit a big cigar as they sat on the stuffed furniture. He and Kline were drinking whiskey. Eli was sipping apple cider, and no one had dared smile about it.

"This will be a city someday," Sims said. "It's not a fast boomer like Tombstone. This town is growing slow but strong. There's a lot of gold here, and some copper too."

"And you'll take your share," Kline said.

"Well, sure, I'm a businessman," Sims replied with a laugh. "But what I want is good for this town. First, though, we gotta clean up the east side. It's wilder every day. We gotta have some law, and I even asked Mr. Cole here if he'd be sheriff."

"And what did he say?" Kline asked.

"He said no," Eli responded.

Sims made a face. "Too bad. I could've done right by you, Mr. Cole. Well, now it's up to you, Marshal."

"If I appoint another deputy," Kline said, leaning back on the sofa, "he won't be your man."

"You misunderstand me, Marshal. There's no harm in makin' sure our peace officer has all he needs."

Doris swept into the room. After bustling about, she invited them to the dining room as she took Kline's arm. They moved into an elegant room filled with soft lights and a long walnut table set with white china on a lace tablecloth.

The cook was a mixture of Chinese and white, a slim little woman who moved quickly, her face solemn. The meal was steak and fancy vegetables with French wine and rich desserts.

Doris carried most of the light conversation. After dinner she led the men back to the parlor and seated herself at the piano while they plunked down on the sofa and chairs. She played soft, beautiful music.

Eli accepted coffee from the cook, then leaned back to enjoy the music. It was all very pleasing— a pretty woman, nice music, a comfortable sofa. A man could be spoiled, and get rich and fat like Sims.

"If I don't appoint a deputy," Kline said, "you and your townspeople should not only hire a sheriff but think about a little self-government on your own."

"And buck the miners' court?" Sims asked.

Doris finished her piece and stood up as they clapped. She joined them and chattered some small talk. Kline and Eli were both glad when it was late enough to excuse themselves politely.

"Best meal I ever had," Kline said, backing to the door.

"You must come again," Doris said. She touched Kline's arm. "I like men in this house."

"And what am I?" Sims asked.

"Why, Daddy, you're not an eligible bachelor, but these men are, aren't you, gentlemen?"

"You must excuse my daughter," Sims said. "She's a little outspoken. Comes from readin' too many books."

Doris fussed over them until they escaped. Once outside in the dark, both men drew a breath of relief. They walked slowly in silence for some time. Then they stopped, looked at each other, and smiled.

"You take her," Eli said. "I won't stand in your way."

"Don't be so generous. I think she has an eye on you."

They walked on until they reached the clearing. Here they paused in the moonlight and gazed at the jail tree.

"Someday I'll fix up that old icehouse," Kline said. "We need a jail. In fact, you could do that yourself and move right in."

"Not me. I'm movin' on as soon as I get what I came for."

"I'm not leavin' till morning. Think about it."

"I'm no lawman."

"There's right and there's wrong. It's born in a man to know that. All you gotta do is turn 'em over to a circuit judge. Come on, we'll take a walk over on the wild side."

As they walked, their heels thumping the boardwalk in the dim light, they thought of the company of women who didn't have to make small talk.

Women who didn't make them feel clumsy and uncomfortable in a fancy parlor. Women who didn't care what fork they used.

Passing the general store, they moved east across the bridge. On the right were the bright lights of the gambling halls. On the left, campfires burned low.

They paused at the entrance to the largest and noisiest saloon, the Golden Lady. Gazing in over the swinging doors, they saw the piano player, cigar in his teeth, pounding out loud, fast music. Men and women were dancing frantically. The men were dirty and grimy. The tired women wore feathered dresses and practiced smiles.

A young woman in a short skirt danced on a tabletop, with men reaching for her. There were grunts and laughter and growls and giggles, and smoke filled the air. Any man here could be Cassidy.

"Bad place," Kline said. "Oughta close it up. 'Course, Sims wouldn't like it. I know he has money in this place and a few others."

"And he wants the law over here?"

"Just enough to protect his take."

They walked into the crowd where a redhead with disarrayed feathers came to greet them as the music stopped. She guided them to the bar, then was dragged off by a surly miner. Two men were now singing at the piano, to softer music, about mother love. The crowd had settled down, partly because of Kline.

Eli and the lawman gazed into the mirror behind the bar. It was strange, Eli thought, to see himself next to a man with a badge. It made him nervous. He just couldn't commit to anything. Not until he found Cassidy.

"Women, everywhere you turn," Kline said.

The bartender poured Kline his whiskey and moved away.

In the mirror, both men saw something new, a gun under a far table in a man's hand. A scrawny miner with black beady eyes was aiming at Kline's back. But Kline didn't move. The man was drawing back the hammer, ready to squeeze the trigger.

Instantly, Eli realized that Kline was not going to draw. And so Eli spun on his heel, firing as his gun cleared the holster. The miner fired into the floor as he crashed back against the' wall.

The gunfire echoed and left a pungent smell in the already smoke-filled room. There was a long but temporary silence. Then the music and noise returned. Two other miners set about dragging the dead man out a back door. The rest continued with their cards and grumbling talk.

Eli could feel his heart rapidly beating in his chest. He had killed a man when it wasn't his fight. It was a new and horrible feeling. He turned and looked at the marshal.

Kline was sipping his drink as if nothing had happened.

"Didn't you see him?" Eli asked.

"Sure did. That was old Elmer. I hanged his son."

"What made you so sure I'd take him? You could've been wrong, you know—dead wrong."

"But I was right."

Eli lifted his Colt and stared down at the gleaming hunk of iron. Eleven men now lay dead. Cassidy would make twelve. Revenge had been all he sought. Now this weapon, this piece of iron, had killed a stranger.

"Well, now," Kline said. "Action honed down, rubber grip, front sight sharpened to a razor's edge. Right handy in a fight."

"It wasn't meant for that old man."

"Never is, but things happen when you wear a badge."

"I'm not wearing one. You are." Eli holstered his gun and swallowed hard.

"You oughta wear a badge," Kline said. "You're the fastest gun I've ever seen."

"That's not enough reason."

"And because you're at the crossroads, Eli."

Kline finished his drink and started for the door. Eli followed, watching in the mirror all the while. Leaving the noise and smoke, he was glad to breathe the clean night air. Kline hadn't even looked behind him.

"How'd you know he didn't have a friend in there?" Eli asked. "He could've got you in the back."

"Not a chance. You were covering me."

Eli made a face, exasperated by this man who was right.

Walking back across the bridge, heels clunking on the wood, they glanced to where the campfires still burned. Gold-hungry men had given up everything to come here.

Leaving the wild side behind, they walked along the main street past a cluster of houses where they could hear a woman singing a lullaby. It made them all the more silent and lonely. Both thought of what other men had.

After passing the general store and the clearing, they came to the Town House. Inside, respectable gentry sat about with their cards. A few leaned on the walnut bar. Sims was laughing loudly at a woman who had struggled free of his fat arms.

At the hotel, Kline turned to Eli and said, "We can talk in my room. There's even a cot in there you can have."

Reluctant but weary, Eli followed. The interior of the hotel was dim and ghostly. Kline led the way up the winding stairs to the dark landing. Inside his room, the lawman turned up the lamp.

They both sat on the bed, and it promptly hit the floor with a crash, taking them with it. Laughing, they crawled off and set about returning the mattress and boards to the frame. Laughter—that was new to Eli.

Kline brought out a bottle of good whiskey, but when Eli declined, the lawman went out for apple cider. Then he poured for both of them.

Still shaken from the stranger's death, Eli sipped the cider. It tasted like something from a barnyard, and he figured it was sour, not knowing that Kline was spiking each glass.

"Eli, how is it a man like you won't take a drink?"

"Matter of upbringin'. My folks were against it. Besides, it tastes rotten."

Eli drank several glasses of the cider. He was slowly becoming dazed, and he was barely aware that Kline had pulled off their boots.

Eli began to mumble about his manhunt, about the men he had gunned on the vengeance trail. He talked of the four who had made it their fight, and of how he had shot them all. Even he himself didn't know how he had accomplished it, except that a man who has no fear is a formidable force. His voice rose as he shouted about Cassidy.

A neighbor banged on the wall for silence, and Kline grinned as he shushed Eli.

"Well, Cassidy ain't showed," Eli muttered, "and tonight I killed an old man I never even met."

"You saved my life."

"You tricked me. All I want is Cassidy, who beat my wife and left them all to die in the fire—my wife, my father and…"

Eli's voice wavered. Tears came to his eyes. He couldn't finish. It was the first time in ten years that he had actually said the words aloud. Rocks were in his stomach. His mouth was burning and his skin was hot.

"So you plan to sit right here and wait for him."

"That's right."

"Without drawing any pay?"

"I still have some money left."

"That why you're bunking in the stable?" Kline asked.

"I like my horse's company."

"You could sit here with a badge and get paid while you're waitin'. Forty a month."

"Even if I took your badge, soon's I got Cassidy I'd leave. There's bad trouble here."

"What kind of trouble?"

Eli lay back on the bed, dazed. "Eve Bennett."

"Every man wants her, but she's spoken for."

"I know. That's my trouble." Eli closed his eyes, shaking his head where he lay.

"Look," Kline said. "We'll fix up the icehouse. The smithy will put up some bars. We'll make a place for you to sleep in there. We'll even cut down the jail tree."

"Not a chance," Eli muttered.

"I'll make it fifty."

But Eli was asleep. Kline leaned over and pinned the badge on Eli's shirt. He walked to the mirror and with a chunk of charcoal wrote in big letters: *GLAD YOU CHANGED YOUR MIND, ELI. MIND THE STORE.*

Then he solemnly administered the oath to Eli, holding up the sleeping man's right hand. "So help you God, Eli," he finished.

Kline felt a tinge of guilt. But it soon passed, and he grinned, pleased with himself. He would make all the arrangements for the new jail before he left town. He'd also see that Eli's gear was sent up.

Kline packed and tied his bedroll, checked his revolver, and walked to the door. He paused to look back.

"You're a better man than you think, Eli Cole," he said softly. "It's time you found that out."

THREE

*I*t was noon before Eli stirred. He was still lying on his back in Kline's bed. He couldn't open his eyes. His head felt heavy and painful. His body was numb, his heart dead. He lay silent, listening. Noise came from the street below, and he realized where he was.

"Kline?" he mumbled. He opened his eyes and sat up slowly. He was alone. He tried to swallow, but his mouth and throat were too dry. He saw the whiskey on the table, but he had not taken a drink. Or had he? Something was mighty strange. His head weighed a ton.

Gradually he remembered the previous night and how he had killed to save Kline's life. He could still see the old man slumped against the wall. He had killed a stranger, not one of his sworn enemies who deserved to die. He had killed an old man who had a grudge.

Kline had said, "You're the fastest gun I've ever seen." Coming from the lawman, it meant something. Eli had never thought of himself that way.

He had practiced every day for ten years, honing his skills,

37

waiting for Cassidy.

Kline had also told him he was at the crossroads. And Eli knew he was right. The road he took now would be for the rest of his life.

Eli noticed that Kline's bedroll was gone, but his own had arrived in its place. He made a face. Then he shook his head, trying to clear it. Kline had wanted him to wear a badge. Well, there was no chance of that. He had no intention of sitting in the icehouse and waiting like a sack of potatoes for Cassidy.

He turned his gaze to the mirror and stared at the words. *GLAD YOU CHANGED YOUR MIND, ELL MIND THE STORE.* He rubbed his eyes and squinted at it again. Then he suddenly remembered hearing soft words in his sleep. What were they? "So help you God, Eli." *No,* Eli thought. *He couldn't have tricked me like that.*

He stood up and managed to walk to the mirror. He reached up to wipe the words away, but he stopped. Staring at his image, he saw something shiny on his chest. A badge! He put his hands on the dresser and glared at himself. Then his common sense slowly began to take hold. He had three dollars in his pocket, maybe a long wait for Cassidy, and a horse in the livery. He needed the money.

Besides, being a lawman would give him exposure. His name would be spread, and Cassidy might come down from one of the mines, or out of the desert, or from whatever hole he was in.

He squinted down at the badge. Deputy United States Marshal. It looked mighty strange on him.

Looking around, he discovered an envelope on the pillow. On it was written, *Deputy Cole, Advance Pay.* Inside was twenty dollars in gold coin, which he shoved into his pocket.

Reaching for his boots, he winced at the pain in his head. As he slid in his right foot, he swore. His foot was resting in something mighty wet. When he pulled free and held the boot upside down, a good pint of whiskey spilled onto the rug.

"Kline, you sidewinder!" he growled.

The lawman had tricked him. All the while they were drinking, Kline had been dumping his whiskey into Eli's apple cider and his boot. And it had worked too. Eli had been too weary and disgusted to pay attention.

Now the rug stank of whiskey. Fine impression of a lawman. He pulled the boots on, after which his right foot squished as he walked around the room. There was a pitcher of water and a towel on the dresser, and he washed his face until he awakened fully.

After checking his gun, he pulled on his hat and went into the hallway. Immediately he stumbled into a pair of haughty women who wrinkled their noses at the smell of whiskey. Aware of his new dignity, he covered his badge with his hat.

Down the winding stairs, he set foot on the floor just as Eve Bennett emerged from the dining room. Her green satin dress matched the color of her eyes. As she turned to face him, her lips trembled with words she had to say. She stared at his badge.

"Mr. Cole, about yesterday, it's just that being alone, I—"

"You're not alone," he said, "but I sure am. Have to clean up that old icehouse, make a jail out of it, and also a place to live. I need help."

Light came into her eyes. "Please, let me help."

"You wouldn't mind?"

"Just give me time to change my clothes."

She seemed excited as she turned and hurried up the stairs.

Eli was pleased with himself. He had found a way to bring her out of her sadness.

Eli started toward the doorway, but paused as he saw the freckled young boy who had taken the marshal's horse. He was about ten, scraggly, and with a hole in his shoe. Towheaded, with a round face and intelligent eyes, he looked warily at Eli.

"You're a friend of Kline's," Eli said. "I could use some help fixin' up the jail."

"You already asked that lady."

"For cleanin', sure, but I need a man for man's work."

"What's the pay?"

"Not a single penny."

"You funnin' me, mister?"

"No."

The boy shifted his weight and studied Eli. Then he stood up straight, grinned, and shook Eli's hand.

"It's a deal. My name's Billy Whitaker."

"Eli Cole."

"I know. I heard how you saved the marshal's life and how you're the fastest draw anybody's ever seen. They didn't even see your hand move. And I heard you was after some guy named Cassidy. And how's you got ten or eleven notches on your gun."

Eli was getting annoyed with the boy, and he started for the door. The boy followed him.

"I heard somethin' else too—that Sims had tried to hire you. He's gonna be worried you went with Kline."

"Meet me at the jail in an hour."

"Right."

Eli put a hand on the boy's shoulder and walked out into the bright afternoon sun. He rubbed his chin and then headed toward the barber's. He passed two women who sniffed the air because of the whiskey in his boots. They were then startled by his badge, and he tipped his hat.

At the barber's, he had the luxury of a hot bath in addition to getting his boots cleaned, a fresh shave, and his black hair cut collar length. Dressed again, he pulled on his hat and studied himself in the mirror.

"Mister," the barber said, "guess you heard about how the lawmen don't live long around here. Maybe you oughta reconsider what you're doin'."

Eli paid him and went back outside. It was hot, and the street was nearly empty. There were a few horses, two wagons, and a few people walking about.

He went on to the Town House, where he sat at a corner table with his back to the wall. He had steak and eggs. Three men at a nearby table were watching him and mumbling to one another.

His badge gleamed in the sunlight from the window. He was getting used to it. He was already used to eating, and it was nice to have a few dollars in his pocket.

He paid for the meal and went back into the hot sunlight. He walked over to the clearing and paused to look at the jail tree. The chains and neck locks lay rusting. He remembered the prisoner of such a tree, a man begging to be shot. A lot of men had sat in the sun in this brutal contraption, taunted and abused and hated. Some could have been innocent.

"Mr. Cole."

He turned to see Doris Sims. She was wearing blue brocade and silk, with her curls tucked up under a feathered bonnet. Even when she smiled, she seemed to be pouting. Surprised at the badge, her smile faded for only a moment.

"Well, what have we here?" she asked.

"I'm not sure yet, Miss Sims."

"Please call me Doris. Where do you plan to live? We have a spare room."

"Thanks, but we're fixin' up the icehouse."

"That dirty old thing? Well, you'll need a woman's advice. Come along."

"Uh, you see—"

"You'll need my help, believe me."

She took his arm and marched him past the jail tree and across the open clearing toward the adobe building that half rose out of the sod. Dust was flying out the door, and Eli hoped it was Billy.

He should have known better. Eve came up the steps and stepped out for a breath of air. She wore a faded blue dress, open wide at the collar, and a scarf about her head to keep her hair away from her throat. She had never been more beautiful. Pausing, broom in hand, she looked at Doris, who was clinging to Eli's arm.

"Well," Doris said, "I didn't know you had hired help."

"No, it's free," Eli said awkwardly.

Doris smiled and released his arm, her blue eyes flashing.

Eve stood very straight, her broom lifted waist high.

"I see," Doris said. "Well, you can't turn down anything that's free."

Eve's eyes were filled with emerald fire. She lifted the broom a little more, knuckles turning white. Doris immediately took the hint.

"Well, Eli," Doris said, "I'll leave you to your work. You must come to dinner again when your maid doesn't occupy your time." She spun on her heel and started to walk away.

As Eve lifted the broom, Eli tried to stop her. He was too late. Eve swung hard and swatted Doris across the backside. Doris squealed, then backed away from them, her face red with fury.

"So that's how it is," she said hotly.

"That's the way it is," Eve replied.

"Well, Deputy," Doris said, "just remember that what you do on your own time is your own business, but what you do on the people's time is ours. My father will tell you what he expects of you."

"He can speak his mind," Eli said.

Doris gave Eve another declaration-of-war look. Then she turned and strutted away toward the bank.

Eve's nose wrinkled slightly. Eli was still in shock.

Billy came out of the icehouse, grinning from ear to ear. "Boy, Miss Bennett, you sure gave her what for."

"I'm afraid I lost my temper," Eve said, flushed.

"You gotta do that more often," the boy said.

Eli turned as the swarthy blacksmith came walking toward them with a sack of cement over one shoulder and an armful of long steel rods and boards. The man was a giant, half bald and looking plenty mean at the moment.

"You the new deputy, eh? My name Schultz. You show me where you want cell. Marshal pay me to fix jail, hang sign. You show me, eh?"

Eli led him down the three steps and into the icehouse where it was cool because half of it was deep in the sod. It was about fifteen feet wide and thirty long. The ceiling was about ten feet high. The only window was in front to the left as one entered.

Someone had already donated a bunk, an old desk, and three wooden chairs. They were stacked near the door. There were some blankets and utensils. A potbellied stove without a chimney lay on its side. Eli figured he could thank Eve for the furniture.

"The cell can be in that corner, away from the window," Eli said, pointing to their right.

"I fix. You just never mind. I fix, okay? Schultz do pretty good job, okay? Make cell. Make lock, hang sign, okay?"

"Well, sure," Eli said.

Kline sure knew his man, Eli thought, well satisfied.

Eli picked up one of the steel bars and went outside. Billy and Eve stood back and watched as he approached the jail tree. He slid the rod in between the chains and the trunk.

Eli worked hard, twisting and fighting, pulling, trying to break free the rusty chains. Suddenly Billy was on one end of the rod, using his weight to help. Slowly the chains began to give. With a crackle, they broke and fell into a heap in the dust.

Relieved, Eli stood back and was suddenly aware of the crowd that had gathered some twenty feet away. Miners with dust and beards were in the forefront. Then some merchants pushed their way through. Sims was in front of them all, a big fat man with a happy smile.

Abruptly, all eyes turned as the smithy tacked up a large wooden sign with black letters: UNITED STATES MARSHAL.

It hit home with Eli for the first time. He felt his face turn cold in the heat. His hands were damp again.

Sims walked over to him and nodded politely to Eve as his gaze swept her figure. He ignored Billy as he spoke loudly.

"Well, we got us a man!"

"He ain't *your* man," Billy said, "and nobody's gonna shoot him in the back like they did my pa."

Sims's smile tightened. "Now, Billy, your pa was a good deputy, but we needed a gunfighter. We need to be rid of that riffraff on the east side."

"You pay the bad guys," Billy said fiercely. "My pa said so. And you get money from the east side."

"You're just a boy," Sims said. "You don't understand."

The banker ignored Billy and offered his hand to Eli, who took it reluctantly in a halfhearted shake.

Sims said, "Welcome, Eli Cole. We'll get your jail outfitted okay. Miss Bennett already talked us into contributing some things, but you'll need more. I got some fine shotguns and rifles I can let you have."

"Reckon I can use 'em," Eli said.

The fat man returned to the crowd, and they all drifted back out of the heat. Billy came over to Eli's side, his face red.

"Why did you shake his hand?" the boy demanded.

"There's more than one way to trap a skunk," Eli said.

"You mean, without gettin' wet?"

"That's right. Now let's get to work."

Before they could turn back to the icehouse, Eli paused to stare at a strange procession coming toward them. A bouncy, plump woman in a bright yellow dress, red hair piled high on her head, was followed by two men carrying a thick mattress.

"I'm Coralee from the dance hall," she said. "I also run the hotel across the street. This here is our best and softest mattress. Real goose down. Ain't hardly been used. It's yours, Marshal."

Eli watched the men deposit their load in the icehouse. He thanked the woman a bit awkwardly.

"Anything else," Coralee said, "you just holler."

"You're very kind," Eve said to her.

"Honey, you're the first woman this side of the bridge to speak with me. You got guts. Take good care of this woman, Eli Cole."

The trio left, ignoring a few indignant citizens. Eli leaned on the tree trunk and tried to drink it all in. People were coming to help.

"They're all afraid of you," Billy said.

The boy turned and walked toward the icehouse. Eve smiled at Eli.

"Are *you?*" he asked.

She shook her head and turned to follow Billy.

The smithy was working steadily, hauling water in and out, mixing the cement, setting the bars, bracing the walls. Eve kept up her cleaning. She left and returned with green curtains for the window. Eli felt that they should be replaced with solid wood and peepholes.

Billy scraped mud from the floor and cleaned out some rotting food from a far corner. Slowly the place began to smell good. Even the dirt floor was neat and fresh. Time passed as they worked, and soon it was evening. Eli lit the lamp that the smithy had brought on one of his trips. The room looked like a home. It was startling.

The smithy stood inside with his hands on his hips. He grinned. "Tomorrow I finish. Fine lock on door now. You no lean on bars. Let cement dry good. Door swing okay now. Tomorrow I finish. When I get more wood, I make you floor."

"Thanks," Eli said, then watched the man leave.

Billy looked at the coming darkness and reluctantly left. Eve and Eli were alone in the jail. Eli looked around him at the set bars, the swinging cell door, the made-up bunk with its down mattress and blankets, the desk now polished, and the curtains on the window that no longer had glass, only a sliding wooden cover—with peepholes.

Eve was standing near the door, broom in hand and dust on her delicate nose. She looked weary. Her green eyes glowed softly as she looked at him.

"When I was a child," she said, "jails were frightening."

She reached for the lamp on the desk and turned up the light. It made her hair look like yellow gold, like nothing Eli had ever seen or touched. She didn't look at him as she moved toward the door. "Why did you take the badge?" she asked.

"Needed the money while I wait for Cassidy."

"Are you going to kill him?"

"Unless he gives himself up."

The words startled Eli. Until now, he had thought only of killing the man. Blast that Kline and his badge. He turned his face away from her as he spoke, his voice breaking:

"He was one of seven that murdered my family. The other six are dead."

"You killed them?"

"Fair fights, every one."

"But the law—"

"My troubles were one problem they had in thousands. I couldn't wait for a few men and a few reward posters. It would only have given the killers time to hide—like Cassidy."

"You could let him go and save yourself."

"He's the one that beat my wife senseless before throwing her in the fire." Eli turned to fuss with the lamp, his eyes burning.

Eve put a timid hand on his arm in a show of compassion.

47

Then she withdrew it, but her touch was still burning his flesh, right through the sleeve. Tears trickled down her face.

"Did I upset you?" he asked.

"I was thinking of your wife."

He swallowed hard. Fingering his gun belt, he looked away as she brushed the tears from her cheeks.

"When it's over," she said, "what will you do?"

"I thought about Oregon and a new life. What about you?"

"You mean why am I going to marry Will Gunnison?"

She folded her arms about the broom and gazed into the night. Her voice was soft, the music gone.

"I have no choice."

"Does he treat you right?"

"Yes, but he's become very jealous."

Abruptly, she laid the broom aside and went up the stairs. Eli followed her into the twilight. They walked silently across the clearing and reached the boardwalk. He walked her to the hotel door and they said good night.

*   *   *

The pleasure of being with Eli quickly faded as Eve entered the lobby. Once again she was a prisoner, lost to all but the cruel threat of Will Gunnison.

Back on the balcony, she stood in the night and watched the stars and half-moon. She thought of Doris, who had all the lovely things that she herself would never have again.

She touched the scar on her cheek, tears in her eyes. She was alone again, lost again, waiting for the return of a man she feared and hated. A woman strong and beautiful to the world, but broken and terrified within.

She turned her gaze to the empty street. And waited.

FOUR

*I*t was his first night in the new jail, and Eli lay fully clothed on the narrow bunk. With the lamp turned low, he could see the empty cell in the corner, its door ajar. The curtains looked strange on the newly barred window over his desk.

Rising, he walked to the window and gazed into the night. The stars blinked as clouds swiftly passed. There was a smell of rain in the air. In the dim moonlight he could see the jail tree, now naked. Beyond were the dim lights of buildings.

Out there, people were together. Even the bad ones had someone close to them. It was Eli who was alone tonight. He thought of Kline, riding out there, somewhere, with a badge for a target. One man in an empty land, also alone.

And Cassidy? Was he out there like an animal in hiding? Or was he enjoying a big dinner with some choice woman? Was he going to ignore the threat of Eli Cole or would Eli's presence grind on him as it had the others, forcing his move?

After pacing awhile, he slid the wooden cover over the barred window and then turned the lamp to the lowest light. He went back to his bunk with his gun in hand. Even here with the heavy bar across the door, he couldn't close his eyes without cold iron in his grasp.

At dawn he awakened suddenly, tense. Then he heard it, a shot echoing. He sprang to his feet, hat pulled on tight, gun in hand. He slid back the window cover and peered into the morning light, but saw nothing.

There were storm clouds in the sky. The first rays of the sun lay crimson on the eastern slope.

Walking outside, he heard loud noises. North of town, at the foot of the ridge, below the first group of mines, there was a commotion. Dust was rising. Eli strode up the street and turned the corner where a great, barren tree stood.

A crowd of miners was dragging a scrawny old man, his hands tied behind him, to the foot of the tree. Someone was already throwing a rope over the highest limb. A nervous horse was being led into the crowd.

Eli walked to within ten feet of the bearded, violent miners, who paused to glare at him. Their eyes were black and gleaming in the early light. Many had rifles. They smelled of dust and grime and sweat.

Ignoring Eli, they lifted their victim onto the saddle and pulled a heavy noose around his neck. The old man was an ancient shell, his little round eyes half covered by heavy brows. His beard was short and gray. He showed no panic, only resignation in the face of death.

"Let him down," Eli said, a hand on his holstered gun.

"He robbed a sluice," a red-bearded miner said. "It's the law. We gotta hang 'im."

"Let him down," Eli said.

The men stood firm. Eli heard movement and voices behind

him. A crowd was moving off to the side where he could see Sims in a green robe. Behind him were other half-dressed solid citizens, standing out of the line of fire. He saw Billy Whitaker behind Sims.

The fat banker looked nervously from Eli to the miners and said, "It's a law in any mining camp."

"Not when there's Federal law," Eli replied.

"A gunfighter talks about law!" a miner shouted.

"That's Masters," Sims said, nodding toward the man with the red beard. "He's head of the miners' court. They don't need or want *your* law, Marshal."

The miners nodded and mumbled their agreement. Masters stood defiantly in front of his crowd, a big man with big hands holding a rifle. Eli stood quietly, knowing that he had to act.

Slowly he drew his gun. The miners waited, daring him to fire in cold blood. The prisoner sat, numb and breathless, on the trembling horse, the noose around his neck. The rope swayed against the crimson sky.

"Let it be," Sims said to Eli.

Masters called out, "You with us, Mr. Sims?"

"I'm with you," Sims said loudly. "Our new deputy doesn't understand."

"Let the man down," Eli said, his gun steady in his hand.

"He was found guilty," Masters growled. "Now he dies."

Masters turned to whack the horse on the rump with his rifle butt. The animal shot forward. The prisoner left the saddle, hitting the end of the swinging rope.

Eli raised his gun and fired. The swaying rope was shattered in midair. The old man kicked and crashed to the ground. He rolled over crazily and sat up, gasping for air, eyes round with disbelief. He still had the noose tight about his neck.

Frozen, the miners could only stare in dismay and sudden respect, defiance gone, rifles lowered. Sims's mouth was open, but he was speechless. Billy was hugging himself with joy.

Now the sky rolled with thunder and darkened the land.

Masters wiped his mouth. "All right, Marshal, you made your point. Now what?"

"He'll stand trial when the circuit judge comes through."

"He's *been* tried!" Masters shot at him as he stepped forward.

"Robbery is not a hanging offense," Eli said. "He took a handful of dirt. You don't hang a man for that."

Sims appeared to know when he should change sides. "Maybe he's right," he said. "Maybe it's time we had some real law. Let's give it a chance so we can get back to our own business."

There was a long hesitation. The miners glanced toward the dark sky and their holes in the ridge. They wanted to attend to their claims.

"Why not?" Masters grunted. "He won't live long, anyway."

There was a long moment of silence. Then a roll of thunder crossed the sky. The clouds were moving more swiftly now.

His hands freed by Billy, the prisoner pulled the rope from his neck and staggered to his feet. He fell to his knees, still shaken. He looked up at Eli with tears in his eyes. Eli took his arm and helped him to his feet. The crowd was still watching. Sims was ready to take advantage of the situation. His ruddy face beamed suddenly.

"Men," he said, "let's hear it for the best darn shot I ever saw."

There was a pause, then nervous laughter. The miners shrugged and moved away. The townspeople took a long look at the new lawman. Some registered approval, others fear or dissent. But there was no changing the fact that there was a marshal in town.

Eli considered the fat banker and wondered again if he was Cassidy. The miners moved away, every face turned back now and then, emotions hidden by beards and grime. One of them could be Cassidy.

Holding a gun and wearing a badge on his shirt, Eli felt a new strangeness. He had just saved an old man's life in the name of the law.

Everyone slowly dispersed except Sims and Billy, who both walked behind Eli and the prisoner. Again the dark sky rumbled and shut out the sun. There was a smell of rain.

"Have to send for the circuit judge," Sims said.

"You change sides easily," Eli remarked.

"Man has to live a second at a time out here. By the way, what makes you think robbery ain't no hangin' offense?"

"You hang a man for stealin' cattle and horses, not for dirt worth fifty cents."

"Maybe," Sims said, drawing his robe about him. "Reckon I'll go on back to bed. Looks like the law's in town after all. But you come and see me, Cole. I can do a lot for you."

Eli, Billy, and the prisoner continued to the jail.

"Stealin' ain't no hanging offense?" Billy asked.

"Heck, I don't know," Eli said.

Billy grinned. They looked up at the sky again. It was starting to spread big, scattered drops.

"Marshal," Billy said, "that sure was the best shot anyone ever saw. The rope was jumpin' and swingin', and it was still dark."

"But he sure waited long enough," the old man grumbled. He

rubbed his sore neck where it was red from the burn.

"Lock 'im up," Billy said. "I got somethin' you'll need."

The boy scrambled off down the street. Eli hurried the old man into the jail and then the cell, closing the door on him with a bang.

His first prisoner, here, in the same room, glaring back at him. A stinking prisoner at that. The stench of the old man caused him to leave the outside door open. Soon the old man curled up on a blanket on the cell bunk and was snoring away.

Eli sat down at his desk and looked at the ledger given to him. He hadn't expected to have anything to write in it so soon. He could just see Kline's self- satisfied smile.

He heard running feet and he put his hand on his holster. It was only Billy, coming down the brick steps and out of breath. He was carrying four huge books. He plunked them down on Eli's desk in front of him.

"There," the boy said proudly. "My dad's law books!"

"Law books?"

"Sure. Can you read?"

"Yeah, but   "

"They tell you what the law is, so you can later tell those men out there."

Eli stared at the rumpled, leather-bound books. He touched them carefully, as if they might fall apart.

"Two of them, that's Federal law," Billy said. "One's territorial and the other is all about court law. My dad said it sort of tells you what the law means."

Eli couldn't believe what was happening to him. He leaned back, trying to stem his excitement. He looked at Billy, still uncertain.

"You don't have to memorize them," Billy said. "You just look stuff up, like murder. Someone robs the bank, you look that up too. Maybe it's even got crimes like robbing a handful of dirt."

Eli smiled. "I guess I did talk big out there."

"You had to. Hey, I'll get some grub for you and the old man. I'll be right back."

Billy ran up the stairs and out into the drizzle. Eli sat staring at the heavy books. He hadn't looked at a book since he'd mustered out of the Army. All he'd ever needed in his hand was a Colt revolver.

Slowly, cautiously, he now drew one of the law books toward him and opened it very carefully. The pages had been turned down many times and were worn and thin. The print was small, and he turned up the lamp, listening to the rain on the roof.

All else faded from his mind as the words sprang up before his eyes. While he read, sitting alone in the jail with his snoring prisoner, he forgot about Sims and the miners and his own vengeance.

But Sims had not forgotten Eli Cole. In his parlor, the fat man was pacing back and forth in his robe, cigar in the corner of his mouth, face white and red and hot, with sweat on his many chins.

Doris was trying to calm him. She was still in her dressing gown.

"Now, Daddy, you did want a lawman here."

"I wanted my own man with a badge."

"But he'll be *your* man in time."

"No, blast it! He's another Kline."

"Daddy, please sit down."

"Didn't you hear what I said? You didn't see their faces. A

lucky shot, that's what it was. All those miners, backin' off from that one gun. I can't believe it. And after shootin' off my mouth on their side, I had to back off and be on Cole's side."

"Daddy, give it time. He'll need money sooner or later. And I'll work on him."

"No good, honey. That man doesn't care if he lives or dies. A man like that, you gotta kill. It wouldn't be murder, just a faster gun, like Decker."

"The man you sent for?"

"He's on his way here now. I was gonna stick a badge on him, but now I'll pay him for something else. Oh, it'll be a fair fight. I promise, honey." She sat down on the arm of his chair. "Daddy, what if I wanted Eli Cole?"

"Play with him and try to bring him over to our side, honey, but he's not for you."

He leaned back and she stroked his cheek. They sat in the luxury of their parlor, talking about the near-hanging, the angry miners, and this strange man, Eli Cole. They also considered all the luxury they would have to give up if the east side closed. While they talked, the rain fell on their fine roof and in the dust. Streaks of sunlight came out as the clouds moved swiftly across the morning sky.

*   *   *

The jail roof was thick with sod and it dripped from the rain near the wall behind Eli's desk. He didn't notice. He was too busy searching the books, looking for words he had heard from men like Kline. Words that came from history and Congress and the courts, and that were set down here in these thick books.

He was alone, the prisoner still snoring. His back ached from bending over the books, and he leaned back. It was then that Billy came charging inside, followed by Eve Bennett with a heavy tray in her hands. She looked fresh and lovely in a gray silk dress with lace and red trim. Her yellow hair was back from her face and damp from the rain. The cape over her shoulders was dripping. She set down the tray on his desk and smiled at him.

"Your breakfast, Marshal," she said.

"What about the prisoner?"

"Later," Billy said.

Eli uncovered the tray and found hot bacon and eggs with a pot of coffee. It smelled wonderful. He didn't look up, afraid to show his pleasure. As he tore into it, his visitors sat down on the wooden chairs in front of his desk.

"It's still raining," Eve said. "It makes everything clean and fresh."

"The whole town's talkin' about you," Billy told him. "You're a real hero."

"You help it any?" Eli asked.

Billy laughed. "Maybe so, but it was really somethin'."

"I wish I had seen it," Eve said.

"No," Eli countered. "You shouldn't see a thing like that."

"That's right," Billy said. "It ain't for women."

"It *isn't* for women," Eve corrected.

"That's what I said," Billy responded, miffed.

Eve smiled and didn't pursue the issue.

Eli felt a grin crinkle his lips open. It came easier. His face didn't crack as much. He felt comfortable here with his new friends. Friends. Eve and Billy and Kline.

Before he came to Yellow Creek, there had been no one in his life for ten years. He had shut out all feeling. It was the only way he could hunt down men. And because he didn't care whether he lived or died, his aim had been deadly. Now he was changing, softening. It could be dangerous.

"I'll take the tray and get the prisoner's grub," Billy said. "You need anything else, Marshal?"

"Just leave the coffee. Thanks."

"You really been readin' those books?" the boy asked.

Eli nodded, and Billy grinned as he hurried out the door with the tray. Eve smiled after him as she spoke:

"He's a wonderful young man."

"Smart enough to bring two cups. How about some coffee?"

"Yes, please."

Eli poured the coffee and then leaned back and glanced at the snoring prisoner.

"You wouldn't think he was almost hanged," he said.

"It was a brave thing you did. I was wrong about you, Eli Cole, and I'm glad."

"Wrong enough to answer a question about that scar?"

She looked down at her cup, shaking a little, and she set it aside. Rising, she moved toward the open door, but he was quickly there, blocking her path. She turned away, her back to him as she spoke.

"It was an accident."

"Gunnison?"

"No, there was a fight over me. I was struck by a broken bottle. Will was so angry he shot the man down."

He stood aside, sorry he had upset her. She moved to the steps, lifting her skirts as she climbed, and left.

Eli had never been able to speak with women without stumbling all over himself, even with his bride. Yet with Eve, it seemed easier somehow. She was soft, vulnerable, compassionate, and warm. Nothing he could say to her would be laughed at or brushed away.

He tried to concentrate on the books again, but Billy soon appeared with food for the prisoner. He slid the tray under the cell door and turned to Eli.

"Miss Bennett sure is pretty, eh, Marshal?"

"Sure is."

Billy banged on the bars. The prisoner stirred with a snort, sat up, rubbed his eyes, and yawned. Seeing the tray, the old man cackled with delight and raised it from the floor.

"Hey, mister, aren't you gonna thank the marshal?"

"Thank him for what?" the old man grunted. "I'm gonna die, anyhow."

"But right now, you're gettin' a full belly," Billy said. "And you're out of the rain."

"You got somethin' there, kid. Thanks, Marshal."

Eli nodded and poured himself some more coffee. The sky was rolling with thunder, and rain was trickling down the steps. Billy closed the door, and Eli had to brighten the lamp. The boy leaned close to Eli and the books.

"They're almost like Bibles. My pa said so."

"Well, not quite, but they're something, all right."

Together they read the books. The day wore on. When night fell once more, the rain and clouds were gone, and the stars were brilliant and close. The pale moon was half full in the distant black of the sky.

That night Eli walked alone in the street, smelling the

freshness left by the rain. Every little sound was louder now, like the clank of a pick somewhere on the ridge. The street was deserted but for horses tied to railings. A few lights from windows sent strange patterns onto the boardwalk.

He found himself checking the doors of dark shops to make sure they were locked. In front of the bank, he paused to look across the street at the ghostly frame of the hotel. There was a light in Eve's window.

As he wandered farther along the street, a woman's voice called to him. He turned, surprised to see Doris Sims. She was wearing a cape and smiling at him from the porch of her house. She sat down on the swing and beckoned to him as he approached. He walked onto the porch but chose to stand. She did look pretty in the moonlight.

"I saw you playing marshal," she said. "Aren't you afraid?"

"Maybe."

She stood up slowly and walked toward him. He backed away, but, still smiling, she caught his arm. She smelled of expensive perfume.

"Why haven't you called on me?"

"No time. Besides, I reckon there must be a lot of other men calling at your door."

"But you're different, Eli."

"Because I wear a badge?"

"You're not a very trusting man."

"That's how I stay alive."

"How can I change your mind?"

She put her hands on his shoulders and stood on her tiptoes, pulling him down to kiss his dry lips with her soft, fragrant ones. A sensation went through him. She touched his face with her fingertips, then drew away from him.

"Don't say anything, Eli. Just come back."

She turned and rushed into the house.

Eli drew a deep breath, her kiss still on his lips. Then, not knowing why, he wiped his mouth with the back of his hand. Turning away, he went back into the night. If things had been different in his life, he might have called on her. But her father could well be Cassidy.

He shrugged, grim with the thought, and walked back along the street to the wooden bridge and the east side of town. He moved toward the lights of the noisy saloons. To his left, the campfires still burned. A woman was shouting at her child. There was the smell of scorched meat. Smoke drifted toward him in the night.

He walked to the front of the Golden Lady, pausing to gaze up the street. There were no men out, only their horses and a wagon. At the swinging doors, he stood out of the light and looked inside. It was noisy, crowded, smoky, and smelled of whiskey. A man was cussing at a poker table. The feathered redhead was sitting on the piano.

He stood in the shadows as the crowd grew quiet, listening to her sweet voice as she sang:

> *"The lonely man walks a lonely street,*
> *No shadows fall at his silent feet.*
> *The blood is dry on his ghostly hand,*
> *For too soon dead is the lonely man."*

The song was as melancholy as her voice. Eli turned away and walked toward the other saloons, keeping out of sight. All was normal but loud and noisy. As he walked back past the Golden Lady, he heard the applause for the redhead's song.

Moving on to the bridge, he glanced toward the ridge where tiny lights could be seen. Men hungry for gold or silver never quit. And hunters—could *they* ever stop?

Straightening, his hand on his holster, he walked back to the west side and along the boardwalk. As he passed the barren tree, his steps grew heavier. And near the jail, he paused. All he had this night was an adobe shelter and a snoring prisoner. Whatever he faced tomorrow, it would be alone, and the redhead's song was ringing in his ears. Too soon dead was a lonely man.

And Eli Cole was suddenly a very lonely man.

FIVE

*W*ill Gunnison drew his big bay to a halt and gazed down the ridge at Yellow Creek. The town was spread below in a clump at the foot of the far rise. His companion was sitting a sorrel.

Gunnison's thin, swarthy face was sober, and his blue eyes were shaded by a drooping hat brim. There was a cleft in his narrow chin. On his rough face was a few days' growth of wiry brown beard. His white shirt was damp with sweat. A long black coat was tied down with his bedroll. His bay gelding pawed the earth restlessly.

Decker, the man on the sorrel, was smaller and hardier of build, wearing all black with conchos on his hatband and gun belt. His skin was dark and taut, and his face looked carved from stone. He had a hooked nose and a tight, thin mouth. He crossed his leg over the pommel and rolled a smoke.

"Thought we'd never get here," Decker said. "I got to see if that woman of yours is as pretty as you say. Maybe I'll take her away from you."

"Men have tried, but they're all dead."

64

Decker laughed, but both men weighed the danger of the other. Decker was known as the fastest gun alive, but Gunnison was pretty fast himself. Decker had the reputation, but Gunnison had the bravado. The difference between them was that Gunnison wanted to stay alive and Decker didn't care one way or the other.

Decker lit his smoke and then wiped his brow. "Well," he said, "ain't never seen a woman worth fightin' over."

"Soon as I get the money I need, I'm takin' her to San Francisco. We'll be married there and live in a fine house on some high hill overlooking the ocean."

Gunnison leaned forward to stroke the neck of his restless bay. He could see Eve's lovely face, the shine in her emerald eyes.

"We made a good haul this time," Decker said, "but this feller Sims takes too big a cut."

"Someday we may just cut him out."

"Well, if he pins a badge on me, we'll pretty much be in charge. And if he's got other business for me, he'll have to pay my price—five hundred a man."

"Whatever happens, before we move on, we take the bank. After I send Eve on ahead, that is."

"She got no idea where you get all your money?"

Gunnison shook his head. He studied his companion for a long moment. Decker was creepy but a good partner.

They started their horses down the slope. They passed a lone, unmarked grave near the far edge of a boot hill.

The land was taking its toll, but each vowed that it would never get him. They rode into the west side of town, heading for the hotel. Because of the heat, only a few people were standing in the shade. The streets were otherwise empty except for a few horses and wagons and a panting dog.

Gunnison glanced across the clearing at the jail tree he had heard about. The chains were gone, but there was a building in the rear that caught his eye. As they reined up, Gunnison squinted to read the sign: UNITED STATES MARSHAL.

"Look," he said.

"That varmint Kline must stake out here." They reached the hotel and stopped at the railing. On the balcony, standing in the sun, her yellow hair glistening, Eve Bennett looked down at them. She was wearing green silk. Her hands gripped the railing.

Decker moistened his lips as he spoke: "You told the truth for the first time in your rotten life."

"Take care of my horse, will you?"

"Long as I get to meet her," Decker said. "That's all you get to do."

"As long as you live, right?"

"Right."

Gunnison dismounted and handed the reins to Decker. Eve had drawn back out of sight. Gunnison considered the hunger in Decker's eyes, and it gave him pleasure to know he had something that Decker would give his eyeteeth to have.

Gunnison hurried into the hotel and up the stairs with long strides. He quickly went down the hall to the room where Eve had appeared. The door was unlocked, and he hurried inside.

Unmindful of his grime and sweat, he gazed at this luscious woman. She was by the window, watching him. Her eyes were wide and cool. He told himself she was glad to see him.

He reached for her and pulled her into his arms. She was limp as he kissed her hungrily. Recognizing her resistance, he slowly released her. She had to marry him. She had to do everything he asked. Yet he had a burning need for her to return his love. He would be patient.

Meanwhile, at the livery, Decker was thinking of Eve. He would think about her a lot from now on.

But as he left the livery, he saw a boy watching him in the shade.

"Hey, kid, where does Mr. Sims live?"

"Big white house, end of town, that way. But he's in the bank now."

Billy watched him stride toward the bank. The silver conchos were for show, but the tied-down holster was obviously for work. He waited until Decker had entered the bank, and then he ran all the way to the jail house. He found the prisoner snoring and Eli at his desk, studying reward posters.

"Hey, slow down," Eli said.

"Guess who just rode in?"

"Geronimo."

"Come on, Marshal, be serious."

"Kline?"

"No, Decker!"

Eli stiffened.

"He's a hired killer," Billy said.

"I've heard of him."

"They say he's awful fast, Marshal."

"Heard that too."

"My pa saw him back down three men once."

"How do you know it's him?"

"By the way he's dressed—all in black, silver conchos and all."

Eli shrugged and pushed the posters aside. "He's not a wanted man, Billy."

"He was askin' about Mr. Sims. He went to see him at the bank. And he didn't come here alone. A man rode in with him, but he went up to see Miss Bennett."

Eli leaned back, his face dark and grim, like his insides. Will Gunnison had come back for Eve.

"Marshal, the way I see it, Sims has got to keep making money. If he figures you're in the way, then he's got Decker here to call you out."

"I don't have to fight him, Billy."

"Could be you're faster."

"That ain't no reason to kill a man."

Eli managed to change the subject, and later, as he let Billy scan the reward posters, he began to wonder if either of the new arrivals was Cassidy.

While Eli was discussing law with Billy, Decker was walking out of the bank, frustrated because Sims was not there. He strutted down the street until he came to Sims's big white house. *A lot of money here,* he thought, moistening his lips. He knocked loudly, and after a while the door opened.

Decker drooled over Doris Sims as she stood there in yellow silk and white ribbons. Annoyed by his stare, she started to close the door.

"Hold on," he said. "I'm lookin' for your pa. Name's Decker."

Sims called from inside, "Let him in, Doris."

She stepped aside. Decker brushed her arm as he passed. Walking into the fancy parlor, he was already counting up the money that Sims had to have stashed away. He paused to run his fingers over the gleaming piano.

Sims was sitting in his big chair and didn't get up. They didn't shake hands. Decker plunked on the sofa. Doris came in to serve them drinks, and then she left.

"Fine-lookin' woman," Decker said.

"Thanks, but stay away from her."

"You're the boss."

"My reason for bringing you here has changed. My original plan was to pin a badge on you. Between you and me and Gunnison, we could have had the whole town."

"And now?"

"Now there's a deputy marshal who can't be bought."

"So we just take care of him, right?" Decker asked. "You know my price. Five hundred a man."

"This bein' a Federal badge, we got to make it look good. Out of town, maybe."

"However you call it. What's the fella's name?"

"Eli Cole."

Decker grimaced.

"Ever hear of him?" Sims asked. "He's pretty fast with a gun."

"I'm faster," Decker said.

"You'll have to be. Where's Gunnison?"

"Where do you think?"

Sims grunted and downed his drink. Gunnison was over at the hotel with Eve. He himself would have treated her better. Maybe there was still a way to have her, and to be rid of Gunnison.

"After Cole," he said, "I may have another job for you."

"Gunnison?"

"How did you guess?"

"I've seen her."

Sims studied the man's stone face and tight lips. He wondered just how far he could trust Decker.

"Check in at the hotel," Sims said. "Stay away from me. I'll let you know when to move."

"I make my own moves. And my price is fifteen hundred."

"What? You said five hundred a man."

"Eli Cole's not a man. He's solid iron."

They talked awhile longer, and Sims became weary of his visitor. Doris appeared from the other room as Decker stood and picked up his hat. His eyes roamed over her a moment, and she flushed. Finally he left the house.

"He leaves the smell of death behind him," she said. "What were you talking about? Making him sheriff?"

Sims merely nodded, knowing how she felt about Cole. She sat on the arm of his chair while they talked again about the day when they would move on to some big city like St. Louis or New Orleans. Someday they would take their place in high society.

*   *   *

At the jail, Eli Cole was thinking about Doris, and her kiss, and how the kiss would have felt had it been from Eve. He was startled from his thoughts by the prisoner.

"Marshal, you ain't never asked why I, Charlie Blum, was down to sluice robbin'. I'll tell you why."

"You can tell the judge."

"I was in to Sims so deep that I couldn't get out. A lot of the miners are in to him. He gives you money and then demands double in return. Even takes your diggin's. A lot of men out there are dead 'cause they tried to fight him. And every time the stage is robbed, you can bet our gold goes right back into his bank."

"The stage from Salerno?"

"Comes through once a week when the Apaches ain't on the prod. Due right soon again. Oh, they always got shotguns on it, but it seems like every other time it heads out with gold, it don't make it."

"Do they ever try other ways to ship it?"

"Sure, even sneaked out at night with wagons. Never made it."

"Anyone ever see the men that done it?"

"Always two men in masks."

Eli thought of Decker and Gunnison, the two men who had ridden in, but he was jumping to conclusions. A lot of men rode in pairs.

"I'm tellin' you this 'cause I figure you ain't Sims's man," the prisoner said. "I've heard what you said to the boy."

"I've been meanin' to ask you. Where were you when you were caught sluice robbin'?"

"Marshal, I didn't have no chance. I had just got into the runoff box and was down on my knees, hidin' and feelin' the dirt, lookin' to see if there was gold. Sun wasn't up yet, but there was a moon."

"And someone saw you?"

"Biggest shotgun I ever saw, right in my face. Feller named Rubinsky."

"So you didn't get away with anything?"

"No."

"You didn't take anything or carry it away?"

"Never had a chance."

"You intended to, but you didn't carry anything away."

"What you gettin' at, Marshal?"

"Law," Eli said, running his hand over a thick book.

"Only law here is what they make up."

"It has to end," Eli said.

"You got guts, Marshal, I have to give you that."

And the old man curled up in his corner while Eli read and read until his eyes ached.

He leaned back as the sunlight from the window struck his badge, making it gleam with a different light.

Eli Cole also felt a different light inside his hard body. Put there by Kline and this badge, it was held there by knowledge, knowledge from the pages of a book. Ten years of killing, and here he sat with a law book. Eli could only shake his head and read on.

SIX

In the hotel room the next morning, Eve sat in front of the mirror and combed her hair. Will Gunnison had just arrived, and settled back in a chair, he smoked lazily as he watched her. He was dressed in a new suit of clothes with a red velvet vest, but was still wearing his gun. They were going to have breakfast and then take a carriage ride. There was a knock on the door.

"Open it," he said, sitting up straight.

At the door, Eve drew back and stared at Decker. The man's stone face did not change expression, but his gleaming eyes feasted on her. Frightened, she backed away.

Decker entered and closed the door, backing against it, thumbs hooked in his gun belt. He watched Eve as she resumed her combing.

"Didn't I tell you she was beautiful?" Gunnison asked. "Eve honey, why don't you go on downstairs? We'll be along soon."

Decker could not take his eyes from Eve, and Gunnison tasted the man's hunger with relish. Let them look, but he would bury any man who tried to touch her. Gathering her shawl, she left them without a word.

Decker pulled up a chair and said, "I talked to Sims. He wants me to get the new deputy. He wants it to be a fair fight, if possible."

"What do you mean, 'if possible'? Ain't no man either of us can't take."

Decker leaned back. "This man's different."

"Who the devil is he?"

"Eli Cole."

Gunnison's hand tightened on his gun belt. His knuckles became white, and sweat appeared on his forehead. He forced a smile to his rough face. "The Hunter," he said.

"I can take him," Decker said.

"What else did Sims have to say?"

"Stage came in this morning with the circuit judge. Gonna try a miner this afternoon, afore the stage and the judge move on. Sims don't want no trouble while he's in town."

They scraped the floor with their chairs as they stood up. Outside the door, listening, Eve became frightened and hurried down the stairs into the lobby, to find a seat on a couch.

Decker came down the steps first. He paused to look her over and tip his hat. Gunnison glared after him, then sat at Eve's side.

"He's lucky I need him," Gunnison said.

"He didn't mean anything. Will, let's leave town now, right away. You said we'd be leaving for San Francisco, that we'd be married there."

"And we will, honey, as soon as I'm ready."

"I just have a terrible feeling."

He took her hand, then looked around to be certain that no one was listening.

"Tell me about Eli Cole."

"I heard that he saved Kline's life on the east side. When the miners went to hang a man, he shot the rope and saved him."

"Lucky shot."

"They say he's so fast that you never see his hand move."

Gunnison grunted. "Stories just keep growing. What else?"

"He's looking for a man, a Tom Cassidy."

"Figures. That Cole's a killer."

"But he's not like that at all. He's a good man." He squeezed her hand so tightly that she gasped in pain. "He got eyes for you?"

"No!"

He relaxed his grip and kissed her white fingers. Now he was affectionate and kind again.

* * *

While Will Gunnison renewed promises of a better life, a courtroom was being set up in the nearby Town House. Sims was puffing about the saloon, taking most of the credit. A back room had been set up for the judge's chambers, and a jury had been selected from a hatful of names. The twelve men sat about, mumbling because the bar was closed.

Spectators—men and women—fought over seats near the entrance. There was excitement. Not often was the judge in town for much more than a wedding or dispute. Killings and thefts had always been dealt with in a hurry down at the hanging tree.

"First real trial in Yellow Creek," Sims was saying.

"It's time we got this town cleaned up good and proper and wiped out that east side," a woman said. "We want schools and churches, not saloons."

"All in good time," Sims assured her. "But we gotta do it ourselves."

"Sims is right," the barber said. "You let too much outside law come in and next comes the Army, and pretty soon we got no say about nothin'."

"But today," Sims said, "we're gonna show the outside that we're more than just a boomtown. Let the judge go off tellin' the world we don't need him, that we're law-abidin' folks. We'll make our own town, hire our own sheriff, and write our own laws. We don't even need a deputy marshal."

"He's right," the hardware merchant said. "Today we gotta look like a proper town. You men there on the jury, you gotta be fair and square."

"Only four of us is miners," a grizzled juror said. "I don't see that as bein' fair."

"The marshal and prisoner are comin'!" a man at the window yelled.

Sims set about making sure that everyone was seated. He was taking full charge. They had elected him mayor, but his only qualification had been his money. It gave him pleasure to be their official leader for the first time. This was his chance to show the world he didn't need a Federal deputy. When Blum was convicted and hanged, Cole would lose face for having stopped the hanging in the first place. Then maybe he, Mayor Reginald Sims, could go about selecting Decker as sheriff.

Decker entered, and walking to a corner, he stood with a smoke stuck in the corner of his mouth.

The banker walked to the swinging doors to see Cole and Blum coming up the street. Cole was carrying a shotgun. A lot of miners were milling about in the street. More spectators were coming to see the first "fair trial" in Yellow Creek.

As Billy joined him, Eli said, "Do me a favor. Bring the law books to the courtroom."

Billy turned and ran back to the jail.

The prisoner, hands tied behind his back, was nervous, and he snickered at Eli. "Books don't mean nothin' here, mister."

"They'll mean something to the judge."

"Judge Stone? Hear tell he's a hangin' judge." The crowd made way for Eli and his prisoner to enter the saloon. Eli marched him to a front table, where the old man sat down with a thump. He saw Masters enter and move to the side. Then he saw Decker, back to the wall, in the corner. Like the dozens of other people, they were watching and waiting.

Sims faced the crowd. "Now we need a prosecutor here."

Masters stood up. "If you're meanin' who's gonna get him hanged, I'll do it."

"You're appointed," Sims said. "Sit at this other table."

As he watched Masters move forward, Eli knew that the town wanted a hanging. But he turned now to take his books from the breathless Billy, and he set them on the table. They looked huge and important.

"We ain't got no lawyers here," Sims said, "but someone oughta speak for the prisoner and make it look good."

There was some laughter and applause.

Eli turned and faced the crowd. "I'll stand for the prisoner," he said firmly.

"You?" Sims said. "But that ain't done."

"How do you know?" someone called out, laughing. "How many of us ever been in a real courthouse?"

"I have," Sims said, addressing the crowd. "And in a few minutes the judge will be here. I want you all to be polite and mannerly."

"Just so we get on with the hanging," a miner said.

Masters sat down at the front table to Eli's right. He scowled at the jury, seated to their right. They were all afraid of Masters and his men.

Masters then turned to look at Eli Cole, not sure what to make of him. But it didn't matter, because Blum was going to die, the way it should have been. Masters had to regain control. He made the law for the miners. It wasn't right to have it jerked from him.

Charlie Blum said to Eli, "You're a fool. Ain't nobody gonna save me from that rope."

"I'm gonna try, Charlie."

"Don't matter much, anyhow. I got no family and no place to go."

The door to the back room opened, and the bartender came out and announced, "The judge is cornin'."

The room grew silent. Through the doorway came a balding man of average size, his face long and set with cool gray eyes. A black robe hung down to his boots. He was carrying a book and a gavel.

"All rise," Sims ordered.

There was a scramble of boots and chairs as the crowd managed to stand. The judge walked to a makeshift bench and sat down behind it. He looked sternly at the crowd. They were hushed, for here was a learned man.

"This here court is now in session," Sims said. He waved everyone to sit down.

"State your case," the judge said to Masters.

"Well, Your Honor," Masters said, awkward suddenly, "that's Charlie Blum. He was caught sluice-robbin'. We was fixin' to hang 'im when this here deputy marshal—"

"Lynching?" the judge asked sternly.

"Uh, well, we had our miners' court first."

"The miners' court is not recognized," the judge said.

"Uh, well, Your Honor," Masters said, shrinking a little, "what happened was this here deputy came along and shot him down, and I reckon that's why we're here."

"Shot him down?" the judge asked. He frowned.

"He was already swingin'," Masters said. "The deputy shot clean through the rope."

"Amazing," the judge said. Slowly he turned to look at Eli and the prisoner. "How does the prisoner plead?"

"Not guilty, Your Honor," Eli said.

"You're speaking for the prisoner?"

"Yes, Your Honor."

"A bit irregular, but then we have to make-do." The judge turned to Masters. "Do you have witnesses?"

"Just one, your honor. Jed Rubinsky, the owner ' of that there sluice box."

"The witness will take the stand," the judge said.

Rubinsky, a chubby, dirty, whiskered man, came hurrying in from the crowd. He sat down in the designated chair near the judge, looking pleased with himself. Sims was allowed to bring a Bible and swear him in.

"Place your hand on the Bible, Jed," the banker said. "Do you swear to tell the truth, the whole truth, and nothing but the truth, so help you God?"

"Yep," the witness said.

Eli watched Sims return to the silent crowd. There was a change in some of them. Respect, maybe. Doris was in the back with a few other fine ladies.

Eve Bennett and Will Gunnison came in and moved to the side near Decker. She was wearing a swirl of lace about her throat. Gunnison was lean and swarthy, and wore a light coat in the early heat.

Decker, Gunnison, Sims—they all knew he was Eli Cole. Maybe one of them was Tom Cassidy. Yet in this crowd of surly men, any one of them could be his quarry.

Masters set about questioning Jed, who spoke freely.

"Well, sir, there I was, just got up. I was goin' out to run the water down the sluice, I was, and I seen this here fella hidin' in the sluice box on his hands and knees. I walks up with my shotgun and sticks it in his face."

"What was he doing there?" Masters asked.

"Well, it was still kinda dark, but I knowed he was feelin' around in the dirt, lookin' for nuggets."

"And then you took him prisoner."

"Yep."

"And you called on the miners' court."

"Yep, that's you, Masters. And we was gonna hang him till that there deputy made the wildest shot I ever saw. Cut the rope clean through."

"That's our case, your honor," Masters said.

It was Eli's turn. With a law book open in his hands, he walked around the table, leaning on it as he gazed at the witness.

"Mr. Rubinsky, you said the prisoner was feelin' the dirt?"

"Sure did."

"And you saw his hands in the dirt?"

"Well, not rightly, but I knew they had to be. He was on his hands and knees. That's all there was in there—a lot of dirt."

The crowd laughed, and the judge silenced them with a loud bang of his gavel. Rubinsky was beaming.

"You mean," Eli said, "there was no gold in there."

"Well, there could have been."

"Did he carry off any of it?"

"I told you, I had my shotgun in his face."

"So all you can tell us is that he was hiding in your sluice box, that he didn't do anything else."

"Would *you?* With a shotgun in your face?" Again the crowd laughed, only to be silenced again by the judge's gavel.

"Will defense counsel tell us where he's going?" the judge asked.

"Well, sir, Your Honor," Eli said, sweat on his brow, "I have here a book of law, and it says all about larceny and stealin'."

"Read it," the judge said.

"Well, sir, it says here that a fella is guilty of larceny—stealin', that is—if he commits trespass and carries away the personal property—that's gold—of another—and that's Rubinsky—with intent to permanently deprive him of it."

"That's the law," the judge agreed.

"Well, sir, the prosecution here ain't showed nothin' so far except that the prisoner was on his hands and knees in the sluice box. Maybe there was intent, but they ain't proved it. Maybe Charlie was trespassin', since he got no home. Maybe he was just sleepin' there."

The crowd laughed, again to be silenced by the judge. Then the judge rubbed his chin, looked at the witness, and asked,

"That true, Mr. Rubinsky? He didn't carry away anything that belonged to you?"

"He didn't get no chance," Jed protested.

"It also says, Your Honor," Eli continued, "that larceny of somethin' under fifty dollars is just petty larceny."

"If he'd had a chance," Jed said, "he'd have taken plenty."

"Well," Eli said, "Mr. Sims can testify that Mr. Rubinsky's mine never paid off more than ten dollars a week. But be that as it may, nothin' was taken, so all we got here is trespass. And there ain't been no damage."

"Mr. Rubinsky," the judge said, "do you claim he did any damage to your sluice box?"

"No," the witness said, confused.

Eli closed the book in his hands. Slowly he turned and went back to the table. He saw the strange look on the face of his speechless prisoner.

Masters couldn't muster a cross-examination. His face was beet red, like his beard. The crowd was one big stare.

Eli had no further remarks or questions, and he sat down.

"The witness may return to his seat," the judge said. "Now I'll hear the closing remarks."

Masters stood up and cleared his throat. "Your Honor, all I gotta say is that the prisoner there was caught in the act. Sluice-robbin' has always been a hangin' offense out here. That's all I gotta say."

Masters sat down, and Eli flipped a few pages of his book for effect. Then he stood up and spoke.

"Your Honor, we're sayin' that since Blum carried nothin' away, there was no larceny. At most, he may have been guilty of trespass. If he knew he was on someone else's property, that is."

Eli sat down as his legs buckled.

The crowd was silent. The judge clasped his hands together as he faced the jury. He gave them instructions that were almost word for word what Eli had said.

The jury chose not to retire. Instead, they mumbled among themselves for a few minutes. Then one of them stood up, a disturbed look on his wrinkled face.

"Your Honor, we figure Rubinsky should've waited till Blum had a fistful of his gold dust."

"What's your verdict?" the judge demanded.

"Well, sir, accordin' to what you said, it was trespass."

There was a murmur in the courtroom, but no one seemed surprised. Masters' face was red, and his hands gripped the table.

"The prisoner will rise," the judge said.

With disbelief, the old man staggered to his feet.

"Mr. Blum, this court has found you guilty of trespass. You must pay a fine of five dollars or spend one day and one night in jail."

"I ain't got five dollars," Blum said. "I didn't get nothin'."

There was laughter, and the judge had to silence the crowd again. His stern face fought back a smile.

"One day in jail for the prisoner. You may sit down, Mr. Blum. I have something to say."

Eli sat down with his prisoner. The crowd was silent while it waited for the judge to speak. When he did, his voice was firm but vibrant:

"I want to compliment the jury on a fair and wise decision. I would have directed a verdict for trespass had they not done so. But I have something else to say to this town."

The merchants and good citizens, the miners and dance hall girls, all sat quietly together in the crowded room.

"Seldom in all my many years," the judge said, "have I encountered a new boomtown such as this.

Never have I found such knowledge of the law. Seldom have I seen twelve men set aside their personal belief and ignore common practice to arrive at a just conclusion based only on the facts and evidence presented."

The judge cleared his throat and continued: "What I'm saying, ladies and gentlemen, is that should this town ever seek incorporation or any assistance from the Federal government, I shall be pleased to add my recommendation. All of you should be proud of what you have done this day. You have seen justice done. Thank you."

As the judge stood up, Sims shouted, "All rise!"

"I'll speak with counsel in my chambers," the judge said. "Court is adjourned."

"That's you, Masters," Sims said. "And the deputy."

The man in the black robe dismounted the ladder and went into the back room. The crowd was suddenly jubilant. Sims always took advantage of any situation, and he shouted, "You hear that, folks? We got us a town!"

The owner of the Town House shouted back. "Drinks on the house, folks!"

With applause and laughter, the crowd squeezed its way to the bar. The jury joined them, all looking rather proud as they received pats on the back. Eli looked down at Charlie.

"Can I trust you to lock yourself up?"

"I ain't gonna hang?" Charlie asked blankly. "No," Masters said.

Billy pushed his way to Eli's side. He was beaming with joy. "Marshal, you done it."

"No," Eli said, nodding to the books. "The law did it."

"You want me to carry 'em back for you?" the boy asked.

"Yes, and see that Charlie locks himself up."

"Wow! Shall I take the shotgun too?"

"Not unless you can get Charlie to carry the books."

The old man stood up and grinned. "Carry 'em? I'll hug 'em to death."

The prisoner gathered the heavy books in his arms. Eli handed his shotgun to the boy, whose round, freckled face was full of hero worship.

"Thank you, Marshal," the boy said softly. "My pa would thank you too."

Rubinsky came to slap Charlie on the shoulder. He cackled, "Blum, I saved your worthless life by stoppin' you."

"And I sure thank you," Charlie said.

The men laughed. Then Billy and Charlie made their way through the happy crowd and back to the jail. Eli didn't see Eve and Gunnison, or Decker. Doris had also left. The show was over.

Masters and Eli walked into the back room where the judge was waiting. Already out of his black robe, Judge Stone stood at the desk as he filled his briefcase with papers.

"Mr. Masters," the judge said, "I want to compliment you on your restraint. It takes a big man to defy tradition and understand the difference between right and wrong. You've accepted the jury's decision like a man who should be a leader."

"Thanks," Masters said, his voice wavering. "As for you, Eli Cole," the judge continued, "do you know why I'm here?"

"I figured Sims had sent for you."

"No, not Mr. Sims. I'm here because Marshal Kline asked me to come. His exact words were, 'I got a new deputy in Yellow Creek that's gonna have a full jail when you get there, if he's still alive.' And Mr. Cole, I'm rather disappointed you have only one prisoner. Of course, I'm also glad you're not dead."

"Thanks," Eli said.

"Marshal Kline felt you were an intelligent and honorable man. Your use of those books proves him right. As a favor to Kline and me, don't waste yourself with that six-gun. You have the makings of a good lawman, and we need a lot of those in the territory."

"We need live ones," Masters added.

"I'll be leaving on the stage shortly," the judge said. "I'm proud of you both. And, Mr. Cole, if you ever want to study law, look me up."

"Thank you," Eli said.

They all shook hands and then the judge left. Masters sat on the edge of the desk and shook his head. He said, "I never thought I'd see the day that I'd let something like this happen. A sluice robber—one day in jail. He'll eat better than the rest of us."

"You accepted it kind of easy," Eli said.

"Man's gotta live by what makes sense. It just sounded right. Charlie got caught before he done anything wrong, that's all. Besides, this town's gotta grow."

"Well, stop by the office anytime."

"Maybe you'd let me take a look at them books."

Eli nodded, surprised the man could read.

"Marshal, about that stage leavin' today. It's carrying our gold. Lots of times it don't make it."

"So I've heard."

"We even tried sneakin' it out ourselves. Didn't work."

"Heard that too. You need to organize."

"You ever try to get a bunch of strangers together?"

Eli opened the door and looked out at the noisy crowd. But he didn't have to speak. Masters caught the idea.

"Yeah," the red-bearded man said. "I reckon there ain't so many strangers out there now. I reckon I'll try callin' a meetin' on the east side. Would you come?"

"Sure."

"You know, Marshal, I hope you don't get it in the back like Whitaker did. There's some out there just don't like any kind of badge."

Eli watched him shoulder his way through the crowd. Men were slapping the man on the back.

Not wanting to join the merrymaking, Eli closed the door and looked for the back entrance.

He knew the law had had a little help from up high, and he felt humbled. He had come here to kill and not to save. His life was changing all too fast. Facing Cassidy was going to be mighty hard with all this law eating at him.

As he headed through the alley and across the street toward the jail, he rested his hand on his holster. The cold iron was still there. It reminded him of why he had come to Yellow Creek.

He found Billy waiting in the jail. The door was open for sunlight and it was cooler inside. Charlie was back in his cell, grinning from ear to ear.

"Marshal," the old man said, "it's just beginning to sink in. I ain't gonna hang."

"Unless you go back to stealin'," Billy said.

"Gotta find me a stake," Charlie grunted. "Or a job."

Eli sat at his desk and studied the old man. "Can you shoot?" he asked.

"I can hit a buzzard at ninety feet."

"I need a jailer and someone to cover my back."

"Me?" the old man asked, astonished.

"Won't pay much, but you'll eat okay. You'll have to bunk on the floor or in the cell."

"You got a deal," Charlie said, excited.

"As soon as you serve your time," Eli reminded him.

Billy was grinning. "Marshal, you sure are somethin', but do you really think Charlie can do it?"

"Meanin' I'm too old?" Charlie growled. "Meanin'," Billy said, "you might not be able to kill anybody."

"Boy, I've killed a few, though I ain't right proud of it. Was a time I was young and full o' fight out there with Sam Houston at San Jacinto. Course, that was war."

"You fought for Texas?" Billy asked. "I didn't think anybody could be that old."

"What'd you do after the war?" Eli asked. "Drifted mostly. Fought Injuns with the Army during the War Between the States. I got shot up pretty bad and was mustered out. Joined some of the big herds cornin' up the trail to Kansas. Cooked some, wrangled, fought some. Life on the trail— that was really somethin'."

"You never got married?" Eli asked.

"Came close, but hightailed it out just in time. There's one thing dangerous to a man what he can't fight, and that's a woman, son. They latches on and won't let go, and that's a fact."

Suddenly tired of talking, Charlie mumbled about needing some sleep and rolled over on his bunk. Almost at once, he was snoring.

"You sure showed 'em today," Billy said. "You showed 'em that the law is more'n just a badge."

"What did you learn about Decker?" Eli asked. "He's real bad, they say, and mighty fast. He's gonna call you out, Marshal. I know it. He's gotta prove he's faster."

"Takes two to fight."

"You gotta be careful, Marshal. All them people, they're your friends now, but tomorrow, don't you trust 'em."

The boy had to get home to his mother, and so he left. The late-afternoon sun was soft through the entrance. Eli sat at his desk and stared at his books. He felt no hunger, although he'd see that Charlie was fed. It had been one long day.

He heard the stage rolling out of town, leather slapping on hides. He thought of Judge Stone. He liked the man. He even liked the fact that Kline had sent him. With a half smile, he wrote his report in the ledger.

When night fell, he made his rounds. The party was still going strong at the Town House, but most of the east side people had left. He could see Decker inside, drinking with Gunnison, and Sims forking out the money.

Eli knew that trouble was brewing from those three, but he didn't know when it would come.

Going in by the back door of the Town House, he ordered a dinner on a tray and carried it back to the jail. He locked and barred the door, then awakened Charlie and slid his tray under the cell door.

"Thought this'd be my last meal," Charlie said.

"Everything's under control out there."

"I wasn't funnin' that boy. I been around. But one thing I was funnin' about, though. I should've married that woman thirty years ago back in Texas. A man gets lonely."

Eli nodded and turned up the lamp. He didn't feel like talking. Instead, he opened the books again. Staring at them, he wondered what was in store for him.

His cold, relentless drive had wavered the moment he had killed to save the marshal's life. Worse, he had taken a badge and saved the life of that old man in the cell.

He was fighting within his gut. He was confused.

But now, when he closed his eyes, he saw the warm, soft face of Eve Bennett, her eyes as green as grass, her golden hair about her face, and she was reaching out to him.

Eli knew he was in a lot of trouble.

SEVEN

The next morning, when the cook brought breakfast, Eli unlocked the cell and Charlie came out to sit at his desk with him. The old man's face was aglow with new life and freedom.

"Bein' alive sure makes a man hungry," Charlie said. "What's our next move, anyhow?"

"Move?"

"Well, you came here lookin' for some feller named Cassidy, or so I hear."

"I figure he'll find me, all right," Eli said.

Eli finished his meal and leaned back to enjoy his coffee. He'd been a hunter without friends, but all of a sudden he seemed to have Kline, Billy, the judge, Eve Bennett, and this wiry old man with the wrinkled face.

"You know, Marshal, I sure gotta thank you for this job. Makes me feel like a man again. When a man gets old, sometimes he just gets thrown away." Eli sipped his coffee and listened to him.

"I was the best danged shot in the Army," Charlie continued. "My eyes ain't so good up close, but if you want me to hit a man's jaw at ninety feet in the dark, he's dead. Up close, well, I can use one o' them belly-bustin' shotguns."

"I hope it won't disappoint you if there ain't no fightin'."

"Marshal, I like peace and quiet, but I figure I won't get none of that around you. I just want you to know I'm ready."

"Well, the good citizens gave us that rifle rack and plenty of iron. Just pick what you want. I'm goin' out."

"You be careful, Marshal. They ain't gonna do anythin' where there's witnesses, unless that Decker has guts enough to call you out."

"Just relax, Charlie. Read if you like."

"Me, read? No, but trackin'—*that* I can read." Eli stepped out into the morning sun. He turned to look at the sign above the door: UNITED STATES MARSHAL. Well, it wouldn't hurt to act like one while he was drawing his pay, while he was waiting for Cassidy to make his move.

He crossed the clearing and stepped onto the boardwalk. He tipped his hat to two ladies who were passing in their finery. They smiled and continued on their way. All of a sudden he was respectable.

Two men waved to him. And a merchant paused to say, "Marshal, you done us proud."

"Thanks." Eli swallowed hard and headed for the barber's. He enjoyed the hot bath and shave and felt new again. Yet all the water in the world wouldn't wash away the blood on his hands. All the respectability heaped on him could not erase the faces of men he had shot in one fight after another.

Out on the street, he saw Decker enter the Town House, and he sensed he would have to face that man sooner or later.

Wagons and riders were arriving in town. Smoke and dust

appeared in patches on the ridge. The sun was brutal. Eli went into the Town House, where he saw Decker alone at the bar.

A few men and women were eating at the tables. The bartender, twirling his long handlebar mustache, seemed nervous as Eli walked to the bar and stood a few feet away from Decker. Eli didn't order a drink, but merely leaned on the bar, gazing at Decker as if he wasn't there.

Decker's face was tight. His hooked nose twitched slightly. A smile appeared on his thin lips.

"Can I buy you a drink, Marshal?"

"No, thanks."

"Reckon you're figurin' why I came to Yellow Creek?"

"You bein' paid by Sims?" Eli asked.

"You are right in the open, ain't you, Marshal? Well, let's just say nobody owns Decker."

"Maybe you'll be ridin' on."

"Well, now, that's a mighty interesting suggestion. But I hear tell there's a lawman here who can shoot a swinging rope in mighty poor light. They say he drew and killed a man over on the east side, just from what he saw in the mirror, and drew so fast that no one saw his hand move."

It was a mouthful, and Eli just looked at him. "Now that makes me mighty curious," Decker added.

"Curious is all you'll get."

"You sayin' if I called you out, you'd back off?"

"I'm sayin' you oughta find a reason to ride on." Decker grinned. "I'm wanted somewhere?"

"No poster on you."

"In that case, can I buy you a drink?"

"No, thanks."

"You're ruinin' my reputation, Marshal. I always buy a man a drink afore I kill him."

"That what you're plannin?"

"I don't know. I ain't bought you a drink yet." Eli shrugged, turned, and walked to the entrance. Just then, Sims and his daughter came in. Sims was beaming. Doris gave Eli looks as sweet as sugar and wine.

"Marshal," Sims said, "we're mighty proud."

"That was a nice trick of yours in court," Doris said.

"No trick," Eli replied. "Just law."

"And law is what we need around here," Sims said. "Let's hope the stage gets through this time. We sent three shotgun guards and two men riding behind."

"And the judge inside," Eli told him.

"Daddy, just think," Doris said, "Mr. Cole is a marshal and a lawyer. What else are you, Mr. Cole?"

Eli didn't answer, and she turned to her father.

"Daddy, why don't you do your business with Mr. Decker? I want to talk to Mr. Cole."

"All right, honey, but you be nice, now."

"What business you got with Decker?" Eli asked.

"Man can always use guards when he has gold," Sims said. "I just try to hire up any gunhand I see."

Doris took Eli's arm and pulled him over to the doorway. "Everyone in town is afraid of you now," she said. "You can go and come as you please. Even the east side knows you're in charge."

"Am I?"

"Of course you are. People are afraid of a fast gun. They're also afraid of men who read books. You're a fast gun who reads law

94

books, so you're in charge, Eli Cole. And that means you're free to come to supper."

"Not just yet."

"Don't you find me attractive?"

"Yes, ma'am."

"Prettiest woman in town?" she persisted.

Eli hesitated, his face darkening, and she pouted.

"You're all alike," she said. "Drooling over that woman. But she's spoken for and I'm not, Eli Cole."

Eli was startled and unable to answer.

"I mix you up, don't I?" she asked, smiling prettily.

"You sure do."

Sims came over to join them. "You finished, Doris?"

"For now, Daddy."

They turned toward the tables to find a seat. Eli moved out into the sunlight and took a deep breath. He didn't know much about women—that was for sure.

"Good morning, Marshal," a man said.

Eli turned and saw Will Gunnison with Eve at his side. Gunnison's thin, swarthy face was crossed with a grin, but his blue eyes were cold. Eve looked tired and unhappy, and Gunnison had a tight grip on her arm.

Eli tipped his hat. "Good morning."

"I believe you've met my fiancee. I'm Will Gunnison."

"You stayin' here long?" Eli asked.

Gunnison was wearing a fine suit of clothes, but his gun belt bulged under his coat. As he smiled, Eli didn't like one bit of him.

"I got business here," Gunnison said. "Can I buy you a drink, Marshal?"

"No, thanks."

"We were in the courtroom yesterday," Gunnison said. "Good show, all right. Have you seen Mr. Sims this morning?"

"He's inside. You working for him?"

"I might. He's the only one in town who has enough money."

Eve remained silent, her face tight with hidden emotion. Eli could see her misery as he recalled her fleeting wish that Gunnison should be dead.

This land wasn't easy for a woman without a man's protection. When she had it, however, she was mighty well stuck with him, for better or worse. Eli tipped his hat and moved on down the street.

Gunnison watched Eli walking toward the livery. "Was he givin' you the eye?" he demanded, tightening his grip on her arm.

"No, Will. Please stop it. You're hurting me."

"All right, let's have some breakfast."

Inside, he saw Decker at the bar and nodded to him. Then he led Eve over to where Sims and his daughter were seated. Sims invited them to sit down, and Doris made small talk about her trips back East. Eve merely smiled and nodded.

Sims and Gunnison talked about the town's potential, but it was a deception and both women knew it. When breakfast was done, Doris was the first to rise.

"I'm going home, Daddy. Miss Bennett, you must come to tea."

"Thank you," Eve said.

Doris left them, and Gunnison turned to Eve.

"Mr. Sims and I have business to talk over. Go on to the store and pick out some pretties."

As soon as she left them, the men were joined by Decker.

They sipped their coffee and talked low.

"You saw how it was," Gunnison said. "Cole's a hero. Decker thinks he can take him, but if Cole won't fight, it's gotta be an ambush."

Decker shook his head. "No ambush."

Sims shrugged. "Well, you're mighty sure of yourself, Decker, but if you lose, we're short a man. I got big plans for us."

"Decker's almost as fast as me," Gunnison said. "Then *you* take him," Sims replied.

"This talk bores me," Decker said, rising. "Just tell me when to kill 'im."

Decker gone, Sims wiped his brow and observed, "That man scares me plenty. Now then, what about the next shipment of gold?"

"Talk is that the miners are calling a meeting. They're trying to organize," Gunnison said.

"They tried that before, but it won't work. Except for the miners' court, it's every man for himself over there. Oh, sure, they tried to sneak out a wagon or two, but that's all."

"Just the same," Gunnison said, "we'd best be careful for a while."

*   *   *

While the two men continued their conversation, Eli Cole was still walking and checking out his town. He crossed the wooden bridge to the east side, where he saw Coralee standing outside the dance hall, and he tipped his hat. She smiled her appreciation.

"You got some time, Marshal? You can come in and watch me

practice a new dance from Paris, France."

"No, thanks. Have you seen Masters around?"

"He's at the Golden Lady. Say, that was some fast talkin' you did at the trial."

"Thanks."

He tipped his hat again and walked on toward the Golden Lady. Inside, he saw the mess from the night before. The only customers were two drunks sleeping it off on a table. The bartender, short and squat with a goatee, was otherwise alone.

Eli walked to the bar and asked the bartender, "Seen Masters this morning?"

"There was a big celebration here last night. Guess they're all sleepin' it off."

"Celebration? They wanted to hang Charlie."

"You don't understand these people, Marshal. They're mean, but they're fair-minded. They got a lot of respect for you now."

"You mean for the law."

"Most men wanna do what's right, Marshal. You let 'em do it yesterday without their losin' face. They feel mighty good about it cornin' out fair and square."

Eli looked into the mirror and saw Decker enter, his hand near his gun. Decker touched his holster.

Eli spun, gun in hand. Decker didn't draw, merely grinned.

But Decker was churning inside. *Blast!* he thought. *That Cole is a lot faster than I am. I feel it. I know it.* Just the same, he tried to be nonchalant as he strolled over to Eli.

"A bit edgy, aren't you, Marshal?"

"That was a fool trick."

"Just testin'."

Eli holstered his gun. "Why?"

"You're worth fifteen hundred dollars."

"To who?"

"Give me a whiskey, barkeep," Decker said. "You know, Marshal, now that I seen you draw, I know I can take you."

"I'm not fighting you, Decker."

Eli studied him. Decker had the reputation of being the fastest gun in the West, but it wasn't necessarily so. Another thought was biting at Eli. Was Decker actually Cassidy? Was this why the man was taunting him?

Decker downed a second drink, smiling even though he knew this man could take him in a fair fight. He hadn't seen Eli's hand move. It had been a revelation. Death walked in Eli's holster and Decker knew it. He spoke again, still smiling: "Aren't you on the wrong side of town, Marshal?"

"There's no wrong side."

"I thought you were turnin' respectable. Well, see you around, but you won't know when." Decker was squirming inside, filled with liquor and new dread. He left the saloon and walked into the hot sun. He knew he had met his match, but Sims would want the job done.

Decker didn't want to die. He had too many trails to ride, too many women to crunch in his arms, too much whiskey left to guzzle. Besides, he wanted Eve. He wasn't one bit afraid of Will Gunnison. He hadn't seen him in a square fight, but he figured the man was bragging too much. Besides, in a challenge over Eve, Gunnison would be blind with jealousy and easy to kill. Decker felt like killing a man—right now.

Walking with the sun gleaming on his conchos, he rested his hand on his holster. He felt his liquor, but his fingers were steady. He saw Eve standing alone in the shade by the general store. Gunnison must still be in the Town House with Sims. The street was nearly empty now from the heat.

Eve looked for all the world like a goddess. Decker wanted her, bad. He'd messed up a few women in his life, but this woman was different. He wanted her warm and safe in his arms.

Decker had an urge to prove himself. This was the way, because he could kill Gunnison and have her at the same time. It would be a fair fight.

"Miss Bennett," he said, approaching her. "Eve."

"Oh, Mr. Decker."

"You're a right beautiful woman."

"Please, don't make trouble."

"I'm not afraid of Will Gunnison."

"If you even come near me, he'll kill you."

"Maybe."

"He's done it before."

"Well, let me tell you how it's going to be. I'm going to call him out."

"You've been drinking."

"My hand's never been steadier. I'm callin' him out."

"But why?" she asked, backing away.

"For you, that's why. And because I feel like a killin'."

Eve looked about, but there was no one on the street. Decker sneered at her.

"Lookin' for the marshal? He's over on the east side."

She started to go back into the store, but he quickly blocked her path.

"First time I saw you," he said, "I knew you were going to be mine."

"Please."

"No use screamin'. It'll bring Gunnison faster, but it might bring the marshal too. I ain't ready to kill him yet."

He grabbed her hand and dragged her into the hot sun, jerking her along. Her golden hair flying, she stumbled at his heels. He pulled her to her feet and hauled her into the dusty street in front of the Town House. There he forced her to her knees, his grip tight on her wrist. His gun hand was free as he shouted:

"Gunnison!"

Gunnison and Sims, followed by three other men, came cautiously to the swinging doors. They all fell back as Gunnison, his face tight with fury, stepped onto the boardwalk. He saw the terror in Eve's eyes as she knelt at the feet of a man she despised. Her hair spilled about her face while her eyes filled with tears. The pretty dress he had bought her was sweeping the dust.

"Gunnison, I'm taking your woman!" Decker shouted.

"No, you're not!" Gunnison roared.

Slowly, carefully, Gunnison backed along the boardwalk and then moved into the street some fifteen feet from Decker. He kept his back to the high sun.

Billy Whitaker emerged from the alley. He turned and ran toward the east side.

Faces appeared in windows and doorways. Decker jerked Eve to her feet and thrust her aside. She stumbled backward and fell. She half crawled toward the bank, dust choking her. Exhausted from terror, she collapsed on her elbow, unable to move farther.

Gunnison was sure of himself. He didn't know that Decker had seen the face of death when Eli drew on him, and that Decker was trying to shake his fear by killing another man.

Gunnison stood with feet firmly planted, with his coat drawn back and his hand at his holster. "Anytime," he said.

"You won't give her up without a fight?" Decker snarled.

"You laid a hand on her. You're gonna die for that."

"Hear that, folks?" Decker cried. "I can't back down now, can I?"

"Make your play," Gunnison said.

Decker laughed, a trick he had to throw off the enemy, to make them think he wasn't ready. And as he laughed, he pulled his gun fast and sure, and fired.

But at the same split second, Decker saw the gun in Gunnison's hand, blasting away at him. Gunnison had been faster, though Decker had reached first. Decker felt the thud of death strike his chest. The numbness and shock threw him backward as he fired and missed.

Decker dropped to one knee. He looked at Eve where she lay in the dust in her green satin, with her yellow hair spun about her throat. He kept staring at her and trying to whisper her name. Then he fell sideways and rolled on his back.

Eve half crawled to his side. Frantically, she grasped his arm and cried out in a whisper: "Decker! Please! Don't die!"

She bent over him, and he looked up with glassy eyes. His bloodied hand reached toward her, yearning to touch her yellow hair—just as Gunnison's boot kicked his hand away.

Decker lay staring up at Gunnison, who was glaring down at him. He saw Gunnison reach down, grab Eve's wrist, and pull her to her feet. Faces were gathering around. Decker ignored them and kept staring at Eve's horror. She had tears in her eyes. No one had ever wept for Decker before.

Then he saw Eli Cole looking down at him. He tried to speak

to Eli, even as the barber, who also served as doctor, knelt at his side. Racked with pain, he grimaced and closed his eyes.

Gunnison crushed Eve to his side, then turned her face from the sight of death. She trembled, helpless in his powerful grasp.

Sims broke the stillness: "Marshal, we seen it all. It was fair and square. Decker was manhandling Miss Bennett there, forcing her fiance into a fight."

"That's true, Marshal," another man said.

"Decker reached first," Sims added. "Gunnison was too fast for him."

The barber-doctor looked up, his face wrinkled. "He might make it. Some of you fellas carry him into my shop."

Two men carried the blood-covered body of Decker down the street to the barber shop. Most of the crowd backed into the shade.

"Drinks are on me," Sims said.

Some of the men followed him into the Town House. Others just wandered away. On the boardwalk Billy and Charlie stood watching.

In the middle of the hot, dusty street, Eli Cole stood and observed Gunnison. Tightly held to her fiance's side, Eve had tears in her eyes.

Gunnison still had his revolver in his right hand, but it was pointing earthward. He looked a long time at Eli before holstering his gun. When Eve fainted, Gunnison caught her up in his arms.

"Mind if I take her home now?" Gunnison asked.

Eli shook his head, wishing it was he who was holding and protecting her. He turned from them and went into the barber shop. The barber was working on Decker. He looked up and shook his head.

"Don't look so good," he said.

Decker, spread on the table, opened his eyes. Through a haze, he could see Eli. He began to whisper.

"Marshal, I went gun crazy, out of my head."

"You'll make it," Eli said.

"Gun crazy, Marshal, and you'll get there, too, if you don't hang up your guns."

"Take it easy, Decker," the barber said.

"My name isn't Decker," the gunman whispered hoarsely.

Eli felt his hands tighten. "Who are you?"

Decker was glassy eyed. He tried to speak, but even the whisper was gone from his dry lips. Then his head rolled to the side. The barber checked his pulse, heart, and breath, and then he closed his eyes.

"He's dead," the barber said. "Don't matter who he was."

Eli grimaced, his body tight as a band of steel wire. It *did* matter. If that had been Cassidy, his search would have been over. Now he would never know.

Yet, deep in his gut, he didn't believe it was Cassidy. A gun-crazy, guilt-ridden Tom Cassidy would have turned his fury on Eli Cole, not Gunnison.

For some reason, Decker had chosen to vent his fire on someone other than Eli.

Crossing the street in the hot sun, Eli joined Billy and Charlie, and they returned to the jail, which was cool inside. Charlie and Billy chattered about the gunfight, but Eli sat down and gripped his desk. Maybe he was also gun crazy after ten years of vengeance.

Now there was another gunfighter in town— Gunnison, who had been too fast for Decker. Maybe Gunnison had another name too, and a hidden past. Someone had to be Tom Cassidy. Eli was sure tired of waiting to find out.

"Marshal," Billy said, "I reckon Mr. Gunnison now thinks that if he could take Decker, he could take you."

Charlie said, "Mighty pitiful the way that poor woman was cryin' for Decker not to die. Seems like Gunnison must've done that before."

"She's real pretty," Billy said. "Why does she wanna marry him, anyhow?"

"Love," Charlie said.

"But what's love, anyway?" the boy asked.

"Sonny, love is what makes women beautiful and big men into fools."

Billy just laughed. Then he sobered as they spoke again of Decker and the man who had killed him.

*　　*　　*

While Eli, Billy, and Charlie sat talking about him, Gunnison was in the hotel room where he had carried Eve to her bed.

Even in a faint she looked lovely. She lay with eyes closed and lips parted, her soft hair about her face and throat. Another man had now died for looking at her, for touching her. This time Gunnison had killed more than just a foolish man who wanted her. He had killed a famous gunfighter, Decker. He felt more powerful than ever.

Reaching down, he ran his fingers through Eve's hair. Maybe the time had come to take Sims's money and rid the world of

Eli Cole. He was planning to do that eventually, so he might as well be paid for it.

Eve's eyes opened slowly, and a tear trickled down her cheek. He stroked her cheek gently with his rough hand.

"Don't worry, honey, everything's all right."

"Is he dead?" she whispered.

"Probably."

"Please, Will, let's just go away from here."

"Not without money and some unfinished business. I have to see Sims, to take over where Decker left off."

"What do you mean?"

"Nothing to worry about, honey."

"Will, is it about more killing?"

"No, honey, not unless that marshal gets in my way."

She believed him, almost, and gazed up at him with resignation. There was no escaping him. There was no life outside this room.

"Get some rest," he said. "We'll meet for dinner."

While Gunnison kissed Eve gently, Decker was being buried on boot hill. The man's name was crudely scratched on a wooden marker. No date was added.

After overseeing the burial, Eli went back to town, left his horse at the livery, and headed for the jailhouse. As he was crossing the street, he was hailed by a short, stocky miner.

"Marshal, we got this meetin' tonight and Masters asks if you could come. It's at the Golden Lady after supper."

Eli talked with the man briefly, but no details were forthcoming. He was curious, and after supper he headed for the east side. He crossed the bridge in the moonlight, his boots thumping the aged planks.

At the Golden Lady, he saw the miners crowding inside. The bartender was ringing a bell. Eli entered and was greeted by Masters. Eli sat on the sidelines as Masters headed up the meeting.

"Now then, men," Masters began, "we've got to talk about organizing. Seems the last stage got through all right with the judge and all them guards. But you know we can't go on trustin' Sims's bank and the stage, not if we want to end up with anything."

"We tried organizin'," one miner said.

"Yeah," another said, "and we got all shot up."

"We have to plan it better," Masters told them. "Maybe a shipment of gold by wagon, with ten or fifteen men."

"If I bypass Sims's bank," someone said, "he'd foreclose on me for sure."

"On me, too," another said.

"We could pay him off," Masters suggested. "Maybe form a cooperative."

"What does the marshal say?" a miner asked.

"Well, Marshal?" Masters turned to Eli.

"I'd say a cooperative might work," Eli said. "Another thing that might work is to let the stage go on carrying your gold but send ten or fifteen men with it."

"What ten men want to leave their claim that long?" one man asked. "Who'd pay 'em for their time?"

"The cooperative," Masters said. "We all put somethin' in the pot."

"I'm willin'," a miner said, "but what about Sims's hired guns? Decker got shot, but he'll get more."

"So what? There are hundreds of us," Masters reminded him.

"We can make them back off, right, Marshal?"

"As long as you do it legal, it's fine with me," Eli told him.

"And if we get proof that Sims is robbin' his own shipments?" Masters asked.

"He'll be arrested," Eli assured them.

"Sims is mighty careful," a miner said. "He always hires other guys to do his dirty work. Can't never prove nothin'."

"You just tie him in," Eli said. "If he's callin' the shots, it's conspiracy."

"And you can jail him for that?" Masters asked.

"Yes, but you need a witness or something written. Something the judge can see or hear. And you'd better be careful. Word's sure to get out that you're settin' this in motion."

The meeting continued, with many ideas tossed about and discarded. Eli grew weary of it, because he could think only of Eve and Gunnison.

"Well," Masters said, startling Eli from his thoughts, "it's settled, then. We all put money in the pot to hire our own guards."

"All that sound legal, Marshal?" the barkeep asked.

"Yes," Eli said. "You men might also think about forming your own town this side of the bridge. But you'd need more than saloons and stables."

"We're a long way from churches on this side," Masters said, grinning.

The meeting broke up after a short while, and the men began to drink and play poker. Eli said good night to their leader and headed out into the moonlight.

Walking over the bridge, he passed into the proper side of town. From in front of the hotel, he could see lights in Eve's room, and he felt a pain in his heart.

At the jailhouse Eli sat down while Charlie chomped his meal. Eli started to study reward posters, but Charlie wanted to talk about Decker.

"I wonder why he went gun crazy," Charlie said. "I reckon it was most likely that woman. Yeah, I could see him lookin' at her like she was candy. I reckon he'd have killed Gunnison sooner, but he had to get all worked up first."

"Meanin'?"

"He was wantin' another man's woman. When a man does that, he can't think straight. He's just takin' a dead man's walk, right down the middle of the street."

Eli shrugged, unable to comment.

"I seen you lookin' at her too, Marshal. If you go against Gunnison when you're wantin' his woman, you'll be takin' that dead man's walk yourself."

Eli shuffled the posters. His face was burning.

"Man can't go killin' unless his mind is clear," Charlie went on. "If he's got a big reason to live, he's in trouble."

"You made your point, Charlie."

Eli went outside. He'd return when the old man was asleep. Right now he had to be under the moon and stars and cool off.

Charlie had hit home. Just thinking about Eve had made Eli hesitant. As he walked, he thought of the curse by the woman in Salerno, and her prediction that he would die here.

So much had changed him since he arrived here: law books, a kindly judge, a trusting Kline, a respectful Masters, and a beautiful woman.

Now he had Charlie's assurance that if he faced Gunnison while wanting Eve, he would be taking a dead man's walk. But it would be more than guilt that slowed his hand. In the past, he hadn't cared if he lived. Now he cared too much.

Eli was afraid that the old man was right.

EIGHT

*T*he morning of the next stage arrival, the miners were not yet on the west side. The hulking vehicle bounced on its leather hinges as it pulled to a stop in front of Sims's bank and express office. Sims was already there, chewing on his cigar, while most of the town was still sleeping.

The driver and guard had transported their cargo and two male passengers. The four of them headed for the Town House for breakfast.

Sims watched them pass out of sight before walking inside the express office, where a customer was waiting alone.

It was getting warm already, and Sims loosened his tie. He looked at the little miner with the twisted arm.

"Belcher, you say they're gonna bypass me and ship on this stage?"

"That's right, Mr. Sims. And they got lots of guards."

"Blast! How long is this gonna last?"

"I tell you, it ain't for very long. As long as the stages get through time after time, they're gonna get tired of payin' the guards to ride for nothin'. Just give it time."

"You better be telling me straight."

"Just sayin' what I know," Belcher said.

"Well, I guess I can hold off until they get tired of it."

"Somethin' else they're doin'," the miner said. "They're trying to form their own town and bank."

"No bank'll go there, not while they got all those killings," Sims said.

"But Masters plans on cleanin' it up."

"Masters, eh? He's the main trouble, is he?"

"Only leader we got. You get rid of him, you got no fight over there."

Sims considered this. "Big man, is he? I suppose he's why some of those people over there are starting to complain about my cut."

"They listen to what he says, all right, and he listens to that Eli Cole."

"Seems like we have to make arrangements for a couple of funerals," the banker said.

"Don't look at me. I'll set it up, but I can't pull no trigger, not since my arm got caught up in that minin' gear. You ain't told anyone about me, have you? Anything happens to you, I don't want them cornin' after me."

"Don't worry. But next time, don't leave their meeting until it's over."

"I told you, Mr. Sims, after the marshal left, there weren't no more talk, so I went home and went to bed."

"All right. Here's your fifty dollars. Go out the back way."

"Just don't forget to act surprised when they show up with them armed guards."

Sims grunted and ushered him out through the back door.

Belcher was right. The miners would get tired of paying the guards once they figured it was safe again. Sims was going to need more of those shipments. His men, led by Gunnison, would make sure he collected some more of that gold. There was never enough.

Sims was going to need a lot of money stashed elsewhere in case he ever had to leave town. Of course, he didn't trust Gunnison, but he had to work with someone, and the man seemed fairly polished and intelligent enough.

Outside in the hot sun, Sims adjusted his tie and smoothed a wrinkle on his pin-striped pants leg. He was a big man in town. No one had better mess with him.

Looking down the street toward the wooden bridge, he saw Masters walking to where the stage had stopped in front of his express office. For a few minutes he observed Masters as he inspected the harnessing of a new team. Then Sims lit a cigar and headed toward him. Cheerfully he greeted the man.

"Good morning, Masters. Stage came in early today."

"So I see."

"But don't worry, I can hold it up until you get your shipment ready. We got three regular guards this time, and I added still another, courtesy of the bank. These robberies have got to stop."

"Agreed. We had considered adding our own guards."

"Why, that's not a bad idea," Sims said. "Adding your own men, I mean."

"We figured that that way it would get through. But we're not quite ready yet."

"Well, my own guards ought to be plenty. I guess you must have quite a big shipment this time, the way you been paradin' to the assay office."

"Oh, we had plenty, all right."

"*Had?*" Sims asked, surprised.

"We sent our gold out last night, by wagon."

"Last night?"

"Biggest shipment we ever had. Six men guarded it. So you see, Mr. Sims, you don't need to worry about this shipment. The next time the stage comes, we'll be ready with a troop of men to ride herd on it. Just wanted you to know you don't have to hold up the stage for us."

"Well," the banker said, biting his cigar, "reckon we don't need those extra guards after all."

"We got other plans you'll be hearing about."

"Now, don't forget that my bank is plenty safe. Hasn't been taken once, and quite a few have tried. It's like a fortress. Your gold is safe there between shipments."

Masters grunted and walked away.

Sims was irritated at Masters taking things in his own hands. Maybe Belcher wasn't such a good source after all. The miners must have waited until he left to conclude their plans. All that gold in a wagon, riding away free and clear—that hurt.

He returned to his house and stormed inside. In a dressing gown and looking sleepy, Doris came down the stairs.

"Daddy, why are you slamming the door?"

"The miners sent their gold out last night, by wagon."

"Don't worry, Daddy. You'll get lots more of that gold dust. Just be patient, like me."

"You never strike me as patient, honey."

"I admit that when I take a fancy to a man like Eli Cole, I can't wait. And I plan to attack, at the next dance. I need a new dress, Daddy."

"You just had three new ones made."

"The ladies have been planning this dance for a long time. It'll be in the hotel lobby."

"And you just have to have a new dress."

"Of course I do, Daddy. I'm the daughter of the richest man in town."

He grunted, then grinned as he sat down in the big chair. She sat on the arm and played with his sideburn.

"Okay," he said, "go see Mrs. Whitaker and have her get started."

"Started? I'm having the final fitting today."

"All right. Now go away and let me think."

"You know what I think, Daddy? Ever since Eli Cole came to town, you haven't been the same. You've even been walking the floor nights."

"I just have a lot on my mind, honey. We got this new marshal, Masters is strutting, and Decker got shot. A man can't count on anything anymore."

"You can count on me, Daddy."

She stood up and squeezed his hand. Then she went upstairs to get dressed. Sims loved his daughter, but he had seen very little of her until he moved here and sent for her. He had been delighted to learn she was as mercenary as he.

But he had plans for Eli Cole that didn't include her little games. In fact, Gunnison was to come by and discuss those very plans. With that thought in mind, he knew the knock at the door was Gunnison. He let the man in and they sat down in the fancy parlor.

"The miners are getting out of hand," Sims said. "So I figured."

"They shipped a wagon out last night. Even Belcher didn't

know. Now they want to supply a big guard for the next stage shipment."

"That so?" Gunnison grinned.

"What are you acting so cool about?"

"Eve will swear I sat up late with her."

"What are you getting at?" Sims asked.

"I followed that wagon out of town. I saw six men take up with it down in the hollow."

"And…?"

"Well, I stuck with them awhile. Then I got all six."

Sims brightened. "All by yourself?"

"They never knew what hit them. I was waiting around the bend with two shotguns. I loaded the bodies on it, gold and all, and turned it back toward town. May take a while, but when it gets found, think how brave they're gonna be after that."

"Brilliant!"

"I figured it'd point less to you if I sent it all back, like a warning. They can only guess who it's from."

Sims slapped his thigh in glee. "I'd sure like to see their faces."

"My horse got put away and cooled off afore sunup. Wagon oughta be pulling in anytime now."

"Six men," Sims said, amazed. "You know, Gunnison, I like you more and more. How about a drink?"

"Sure."

Sims filled two glasses and handed one to Gunnison. He had a lot of respect for this man, but since he couldn't have Eve while Gunnison was around, sooner or later the man had to go.

"To Yellow Creek," the banker said. "It'll soon be all ours."

116

They drank the toast. Then Sims spoke again.

"My offer to Decker is yours now if you can take Cole."

"I can take him anytime you say."

"We got to play it slow and keep our hands looking clean. You sure you're covered for last night?"

"Eve's still asleep. I put something in her coffee last night at dinner, something a doctor gave me once. I've used it before."

"You don't trust her?"

"You can't trust any woman," Gunnison said. "Just keep her away from Cole."

"He got eyes for her too?"

"No, the other way around."

"What are you gettin' at?" Gunnison demanded. "When he was fixing up the jail, she was there helping. She even ran my daughter off like he was hers."

Gunnison leaped to his feet, dark with rage. "Hold it," Sims said. "Nothing happened. But next time, don't go leaving a woman like that alone for so long. Any man would want her."

"You too?"

"Not while you're around," Sims said, grinning. "Meaning?"

"Meaning if you and Cole wiped each other out, she'd be all by her lonesome."

"I'd climb outta my grave afore I'd let you put a hand on her. I ain't leavin' her behind for anyone. If I get it, she does too."

"Be sensible, man. You couldn't kill her."

"I read once where the ancients took their women with 'em, and some even took horses and slaves."

"Well, I know you couldn't lay a hand on her," Sims said.

"I already have. You see that scar on her face?"

"You did that?" Sims asked, startled.

"Had to. Do you know what it's like to have a perfect woman? I made her imperfect. Besides, I was drunk and two men had been fighting over her. I killed them both and fixed her for good. But now men want her even more."

Gunnison walked to the doorway, then turned to glare at Sims.

"Just remember what I said, Sims. You don't even think about her! Understand?"

Gunnison stormed out, and Sims heard the front door slam. Sims drew a deep breath of disbelief. He sat and pondered about a man who could shotgun six men and cut his own woman's face without any regret.

*   *   *

While Sims went on to consider how to handle Gunnison, the man's handiwork was coming into town. The horse headed for the livery with six dead men spilled all over the wagon of gold, blood dry on their clothes and faces. The horses were panting, exhausted and hungry, as they pulled the wagon onto the main street.

Crowds gathered from both sides of town as word spread. Masters arrived, and he stared down at the corpses as another miner held the horses. His face was dark with fury, because he was certain that they had been betrayed by one of his men. The only other possibility was that the men had been seen leaving.

' He reached in and pushed a body on its side. The gold was still there. It was a brutal warning. The only one with an interest in regular shipment was Sims, who charged a high percentage for handling through his bank.

Two women came to the wagon, and they wept and hugged each other as they saw their dead men. Masters moved through the crowd as Eli approached. They faced each other away from the clamor.

"Well, we tried," Masters said. "Sent a wagon and six men out last night. They're all dead and the gold's still there. A clear-cut warnin'."

"Must have been a gang."

"Maybe, but they all got it with shotguns. Never knew what hit 'em. Guns are still in their holsters. Rifles not even cocked. It's gotta stop before my side of town comes over here and wipes out yours."

"Just take it easy. I'll ride out and look for sign."

"You do that, Marshal."

Eli went to the wagon to see the dead. He grimaced and turned to the livery stable to get his horse. The miners had not trusted him with their plan, but if they had, he might have been blamed. Just the same, six men were dead.

He saddled his roan and rode out the back way, picking up the wagon trail. If he didn't have any luck, he'd get old Charlie, who claimed to be a tracker. Right now, though, he wanted to be on his own.

If the miners refused to ship by a stage that Sims controlled, they would have to take chances and more would be killed. They should have stayed with the idea of hiring extra guards for the stage.

It took hours before he reached the spot where the wagon had rounded a bend. He dismounted and checked the brush above. There was sign of one man and one horse.

Eli shook his head at the thought of one man brutal enough

to shotgun six fellow beings. Whoever it was had carefully brushed out his trail, and there was no obvious sign that the killer had come to or from Yellow Creek. Once his horse made the main trail, his prints would be lost among others.

By early afternoon Eli was on the east side and entering the Golden Lady, where he asked if Masters was around.

"He's up at the buryin'," the barkeep said.

"Just tell him I was here."

Eli went back into the street and saw Coralee standing in the shade by the dance hall. She was in a yellow satin dress.

"Hi, Marshal. Bad day in Yellow Creek, isn't it?"

"Anyone see the wagon leave?"

"Not sure. We had a few late customers, but no one said anything. Marshal, you never visit us."

"Too much on my mind."

Eli walked back across the bridge, where he saw the stage pulling out with one guard on board and two men riding behind. Only a few people were on the street now. He crossed to the clearing where Charlie was just leaving the jail.

"You got company, Marshal. I figured I'd go have some grub at the Town House."

Eli wasn't in the mood for company. Walking into the jail and down the steps, he welcomed the cool of the adobe shelter. When his eyes became accustomed to the dim light, he saw Eve Bennett leaning on the bars of the empty jail. Her green satin dress matched her eyes, and Eli's breath was taken away. Even with that scar she was unbelievably lovely.

"I came because you might have been wondering where my fiancé was at the time the wagon left town."

"I was wonderin', yes."

"He was with me, Marshal."

"He sent you to tell me this?"

"No."

"Did you know the wagon left at three in the morning?"

Startled, she stared at him. Torn between propriety and her story, she couldn't speak. It was obvious that she didn't want him to think she had been with Gunnison so late at night.

"I thought it left before midnight," she said.

"Were you with Gunnison at three in the morning?"

She shook her head. "I was so sleepy at dinner that I retired early. I guess I don't really know where Will was after that."

Her peach-colored skin had turned red. Then she turned and walked into the jail cell, and this disturbed Eli. He was transfixed by this image, a breathtaking woman framed by slick, cold bars.

"Eve, why don't you leave him?" he asked quietly.

She pressed to the bars that separated them.

"I'm afraid," she said.

"I'd help you."

"You don't understand. He can have my father hanged just by having his friends swear a gunfight wasn't fair. My father is old and sick."

"There's got to be a way to get you out of it."

Her trembling hand went to the scar on her cheek. Then she gripped the bars again with both hands, pressing against them as if trying to reach him. He sensed she wanted to come to him but needed the bars to keep them apart. The thought tore at him.

Eli set one hand near hers. He wanted to be closer, to feel her against him even through the cold steel. He slid his hand over to cover hers.

She winced but didn't withdraw from his grasp.

His big hand closed tighter, feeling the softness of hers, trying to stop her trembling. Her eyes glistened. Words shivered unspoken on her lips.

"Eli Cole," she whispered finally.

He swallowed hard and put his free hand on her other one. They stood silently, his big fingers closed over her small hands. The steel bars kept them apart even as she pressed against them.

"Please," she said, "don't let him kill you."

Tears filled her eyes. He could see that she had been hurt beyond endurance. He was torn up inside with her nearness, and knifed by the longing he thought he saw in her eyes.

"Well," Doris said from the doorway, "isn't that sweet?"

Eli released Eve's hands and turned to look at Doris.

"Go ahead," Doris said, entering with a sweep of pink silk. "Lock her up. Maybe that way nobody else will get shot down because of her. Like you, Eli Cole, if her fiance knew she was here."

Eve withdrew and came out of the cell. She avoided Eli's gaze as she said softly, "Miss Sims is right. I don't belong here."

Eli watched her go up the steps and into the sunlight. Doris danced around him and faced his desk. Reluctantly, he sat down and watched her flirt with him. She twirled her parasol as she smiled.

"Why don't you concentrate on *unattached* women, Marshal?"

"Because she needs help and you don't, Miss Sims."

"I'm Doris, remember? I just want to tell you we're planning a big dance one day soon, and I insist that you come."

"If I can. Now, if you'll excuse me, I'm right busy."

"All you think about is that badge and those miners, and that woman. And those law books. And your six-gun."

"Look, I have work to do."

"My daddy always told me that if I wanted something, I should fight for it. I've got my eye on you, Eli."

Eli leaned back. "I'm mighty busy, Miss Sims." She strolled to the door and smiled prettily. "You know, Marshal, that woman is scared to death of her man. One way she can get rid of him is to have him shot. Are you sure she hasn't got you marked as his executioner?"

"Good-bye, Miss Sims."

She blew him a kiss and disappeared up the steps.

Eli was shaken by her words. He didn't believe for a moment that Eve was instigating a shootout, but it was true enough that he might be facing Gunnison.

Sitting alone, his hands gripping the posters tightly, he thought back to Eve behind the cell bars, bars that represented the prison Gunnison had her in, keeping her from him.

Charlie was right. If he faced Gunnison, he could be taking that dead man's walk.

NINE

Quite satisfied that she had torn Eli apart, Doris went home. She found her father in the parlor, drinking. She sat down on the arm of his chair and kissed him on the cheek.

"Daddy, why are you so upset?"

"At first I figured it was a good idea, sending the bodies back with the gold. Then I saw the faces of the dead, shot up so bad you couldn't tell who was who. There's a lot of furor out there now. Honey, I tell you, it may have split this town."

"It always *was* split."

"But we lived together. Now there's something brewing. But mostly I'm worried about Gunnison. He's crazy. I hope Cole shoots him down."

"You should have seen Eli Cole in the jail, holding hands with Eve Bennett," Doris said, pouting. "You're joshing me."

"No, Daddy, it was real romantic. But after she left, I fixed her wagon. I told him she was just looking for some poor fool to get her free of Gunnison." Sims grimaced, not liking what he heard, but he was thinking ahead now. The woman he wanted was Eve Bennett, and he knew how he would get her. He'd promise her safety, peace, quiet, and riches.

"I'll be glad when we leave for St. Louis," Doris said.

*   *   *

As Doris and Sims talked about the future, Eli, sitting in the jailhouse, was wondering about it too.

Charlie was snoring on the cot in the cell. He slept an awful lot, but then he was awful old. Just the same, he seemed able to move and think mighty fast when he wanted to.

Hearing a noise at the door, Eli looked up to see the little miner with the twisted arm. Masters was shoving him down the steps.

"This here's Belcher," Masters said. "We just found out that Sims is payin' him to spy on us."

"But I don't know nothin'," Belcher said. "I didn't know about the wagon. Nobody tole me. I went home afore they ever talked about it."

"That's true enough," Masters said, "but you could have been listening outside."

"Marshal," Belcher said, "I don't know nothin'. I told Sims about the meetin' and got me fifty dollars for it, money I needed. Look at me with this mangled arm. I ain't good for nothin'."

"Lock him up," Masters said.

"On what evidence?" Eli asked. "You got something the judge would look at?"

"What about that word you was once usin'— conspiracy."

"Marshal," Belcher said, "they want to kill me. Maybe you'd better lock me up for tonight."

"All right," Eli said, nodding to Charlie, who was awake now.

"I hope you can play checkers," Charlie said. He locked the cell on the man. "I can't get a game here nohow."

Masters sat down and faced Eli across his desk.

"We found out about it from one of the women at the dance hall. He was drunk and braggin' where he got his money."

"Right sorry," Eli said. "Dirt sure can rub off on people. I'm willing to bet that before he lost his arm, Belcher there was a good man. And then Sims got to him."

"You're right," Belcher called from the cell. "I was a good man afore I got useless and kicked around. I got me a thirst after that, 'cause I had nothin' to live for. Sims started flashin' his money around. I never did tell him anything that mattered much about the gold shipment. I never got them men killed."

"And you didn't know about the wagon?" Eli asked.

"Even if I had, them was my friends," Belcher said. "I never would've told on 'em. I've just been feedin' Sims a lot of nothin'."

Masters shrugged. "I almost believe him."

"He's safer in jail," Eli said.

"You find anything when you rode out?" Masters asked.

"One man did it, but he covered his tracks well and left enough empty shells for two shotguns, maybe three."

Masters made a face. "Mean varmint."

"Are you keeping a lid on the east side?"

"They're mad over there. I'm tryin' to hold 'em down. They're waitin' for your law and order, but they won't wait long."

Belcher had curled up on the cell cot to sleep it off. Charlie sat on a corner chair, puffing on a smoke.

Masters asked Eli, "What are you plannin' now?"

"Figure I'll ride out overnight and take another look."

"Then let me put a man in here with Charlie tonight."

"I don't need no nursemaid," the old man grunted.

"You might if the whole east side comes over," Eli said.

"Puttin' a man in here," Masters said, "will show that our interests are bein' protected."

"Get me a checker player," Charlie said, sitting on Eli's bunk. "Reckon I can sleep here if you're gone tonight, Marshal."

"I'll get Elms to come," Masters said. "His claim played out and he could use a few dollars."

"But you be careful, Marshal," Charlie said.

"That feller with the shotguns could be out there waitin' for you."

Eli shrugged off the warning, but he knew that the old man was right.

When Masters finally brought old Elms over to sit with Charlie, Eli went to the livery with his bedroll, some grub, and a rifle. He saddled his roan stallion and slid his rifle into the scabbard.

Night was falling as he rode out of town and turned south. He was going to make a wide circle. Somewhere out there he might find tracks or a sign. Or someone might be waiting, as Charlie had said.

While Eli rode toward the night, Charlie was ordering food. When it arrived, he shoved it under the cell door and yelled at the prisoner, "Wake up, you dried-up old coot!"

Belcher jerked and sat up bleary eyed. "That's a fine way to wake a man up. I oughta poke you in the nose."

Both men tugged at their whiskers and growled some more before settling down to eat. Charlie was sitting in Eli's chair, helping himself to his hot food.

"You play checkers?" Charlie asked as he finished.

"I'm the champ around here," Belcher said.

Charlie barred the door and pulled up a chair by the cell bars. He placed a board on his knees with the checkers laid out. Belcher stuck his hands through and made the first move.

For hours they played, arguing and fighting.

Then a knock on the door interrupted them, and Charlie rose to let in Elms. The miner was a big brute with a full beard and long hair, and he looked like a wild man.

Elms was content to sit at the desk and listen to the checker game. Soon Charlie was asleep on Eli's bunk and Belcher was curled up in the cell. Elms was taking first watch.

When he heard them both snoring, Elms looked out through the hole in the door. In his pocket was more than the five dollars Masters had given him to stay here tonight. Elms had taken a little side trip through the back door at Sims's express office, and now he had a thousand dollars in his pocket, enough to get him to another town and grubstake him to new diggings. He would disappear in some other boomtown.

He had taken advantage of Sims's desire to keep the pot boiling in Yellow Creek. Elms had given him bits of news before, not knowing that Belcher was also feeding Sims.

Satisfied that Charlie was in a deep sleep, Elms took up the keys to the cell and quietly unlocked the door. Then he drew a long knife from his boot and bent over the snoring Belcher. With a fierce thrust, he shoved the knife into the old miner's chest. Belcher gasped, horror in his wide-open eyes as he clawed at the air. Elms smashed his face with a fist, silencing his cry. The old man collapsed and died instantly.

Elms wiped his knife clean on the body and shoved the blade back into his boot. He came out of the cell as Charlie began to awaken. Grabbing his rifle, Elms clubbed Charlie on the head repeatedly. Frantic, Charlie tried to rise from the bunk, but was knocked unconscious. Elms drew back, figuring Charlie was going to die.

After blowing out the lamp, he took up his rifle and unbarred the door in the dark. Slipping into the moonlight, he crossed the clearing alongside the general store. The street was empty. It was after midnight. He walked as casually as possible.

His horse and pack mule were tied behind the livery in a corral. Leaving the gate open, he went to his sorrel.

Elms put his hand on his shirt pocket where the money was stashed. Grinning to himself, he pulled his coat from the saddle horn and started to pull it over his big body.

Pausing, he tensed. He thought he heard something. He turned and saw the moonlight on Charlie's rifle. Dropping his coat, he raised his own rifle in a wild frenzy. Charlie fired first.

Elms staggered back from the impact of Charlie's bullet. He stared at Charlie as he dropped to his knees.

The sound of voices and running feet came to them, some from across the wooden bridge, others from the Town House.

Elms gave a last gasp and died before he hit the ground, spread out on his back, still clutching his shirt, staring at the stars in the black sky.

Masters came over to Charlie's side. Blood was running down Charlie's face from the great gashes on his head and brow.

"What happened?" Masters cried.

"He killed Belcher," Charlie said. "Near got me too, but I got a pretty hard head."

Masters was furious and swore mightily. Then he bent down and withdrew the thousand dollars from Elms's shirt pocket.

There was little doubt where it came from, but proof was something else.

"Now we'll never get Sims," a miner said.

"Not as long as Sims got all that money," Masters agreed. "He'll just keep buyin' someone off."

"Then let's get his money," a stubby miner said.

"Let's clean out the west side," another chimed in.

Charlie looked at the faces of the fifty or more miners, their anger hot, their fists clenched.

"No," Masters said. "Just Sims."

"Bleedin' us dry, he was," a miner said. "Then robbin' us too."

"Let's get 'im!" a short miner urged, rifle in hand.

"The bank and the express office, that first," the stubby miner yelled. "He owns most everythin' else. Let's wipe 'im out!"

"Let's go right to Sims's house," the short miner said.

"No, get the gold first!" the stubby man insisted.

"Hold on!" Masters roared above the din. "Wait till mornin'. The marshal should be back then.

And, like he says, we need somethin' to show the judge."

The miners ignored him. They were out of control, and they rushed from the livery and headed for the street.

"Wait!" Charlie called out. "No fires! You'll get innocent people."

"All we want is Sims," one of the men shouted.

Charlie shot his rifle in the air, trying to stop them, but they ignored him and charged forward to the street like wild animals. Nothing was going to stop them.

Masters ran forward to face them, but they knocked him over. Charlie came to his side, and the red-bearded man stood up awkwardly.

The crowd hurtled through the sleeping town. They managed to scrape up torches. Tempers flaring, frustrated, hate gone wild, they moved toward the bank.

Charlie, still dazed and bleeding, grimaced. He had failed Eli Cole. Failed because he was too old. After making sure that Elms was dead, he and Masters set out along the wild street, not sure what they could do.

*   *   *

While the crowd was battering down the bank door, Sims and his daughter were in a wagon behind the hotel. Their most precious belongings and most of the gold were in the back. The big horses in harness were half asleep. The night was cold.

They could hear the thunder of the angry crowd.

Sims had been prepared for just such a disaster should his plan not work. If Elms had gotten away, he would have simply returned the gold. Now he figured that Elms must have talked before he was shot. They'd be after him.

"Daddy, you were right," Doris whispered.

"Sounds like they already got in the bank."

"I'm frightened."

"Don't be. If they find us, we'll just say we had to light out to save ourselves and the town money. We'll get away with it, honey."

"But, Daddy, I'm afraid."

He set the team to moving quietly out of town behind the buildings. They could see fire pouring from the bank. The angry crowd was loud and fierce.

"They won't even know we're gone for a couple of hours,"

Sims said. "We'll sneak out through the canyons and drag brush to cover our tracks. By mornin' we'll be clear and free."

"But they'll keep looking."

"By then, we'll have made it to that rendezvous with three of my old friends. We'll be all right once we get to St. Louis."

From the hillside, they could see flames spurting from the express office. Doris put a hand to her face.

"Oh, Daddy! Now our house is on fire. My piano!"

"Don't you mind, honey. We got enough to buy you a house full of pianos."

Sims kept the team moving toward the canyon, the pale moonlight guiding them. Now and then he looked back at the spreading fires.

His only regret was that he didn't have a chance to take Eve away from Gunnison. All it would have taken was a bullet in Gunnison's back in some dark alley.

"I wish I'd had more time with Eli," Doris said.

"I got my regrets too."

Sims considered his instructions to Gunnison. The man was to meet him in St. Louis if Sims had to leave. That meant he would have another chance at Eve if Gunnison followed through. He knew Gunnison would want his money. Maybe all was not lost.

They were in the canyon now, horseshoes clanging on rocks. Losing sight of the fires in town, they looked only forward now. As they came out of the canyon, Sims reined up short. There in the pale moonlight was Eli Cole. The lawman sat on his big roan, rifle in hand, waiting in their path.

Sims caught his breath, almost at a loss for words. Then he recovered and talked wildly:

"Marshal, you'd best get to town. The miners have gone wild. We just got away with our hides. We'll go on down to Salerno and wait. You can send for us when it's safe."

"What set 'em off?" Eli asked.

"That Elms. He was sent in to help at the jail, but he killed Belcher and Charlie, too, most likely. Someone warned us just in time that the miners were goin' wild."

"Why would Elms kill anyone?"

"Oh, Marshal," Doris said, "you can find all that out when you get there. Please try to save our house."

"I get the blame for everything," Sims said. "That's why we lit out."

"We'll all ride back," Eli said.

"You're crazy!" Sims cried. "They'll kill me!"

"No, they won't. Now turn that wagon around." Sims hesitated and stared into Eli's rifle barrel. "Eli," Doris pleaded, "you've got to let us go where it's safe. You'll get us killed."

"Get movin'," Eli ordered.

"You don't scare me, Marshal," Sims said. "You wouldn't shoot me in cold blood."

"Don't bet on it."

Sweat on his face, Sims turned the wagon around. Eli rode behind them as they went back through the canyon and started down the hillside.

The west side of town was all on fire. As they drew near, they heard screams and shouts and gunfire.

"Marshal, you can't make us go in there," Sims said.

"Circle the town and head for the jail!" Eli told him.

Sims obeyed reluctantly. The town was all lights and smoke, a rash of red and white flames reaching toward the black sky.

Crowds milled around in the streets. Women and children huddled near the hotel, the only building not burning yet.

Sims squirmed on the wagon seat and thought about the gold he had already shipped to himself in St. Louis. Even if he had to get away by himself, he'd be all right once he reached that city. He wasn't worried about Doris. She was resourceful and would join him later.

Circling behind where crazy white flames leaped from red-hot buildings, they managed to get to the jailhouse, which was adobe with a sod roof and not on fire. Sims pulled the wagon to a halt as Eli dismounted.

"What about our things?" Doris asked.

"Just bring what you need," Eli told her.

Sims reached down to grab the carpetbag full of paper money that was stuffed under his shirts. The gold was in the false bottom of the wagon, under their trunks. Doris took her bag of toiletries and clothes. The town was a flaming beacon in the night. People were still screaming. They could hear gunfire.

Eli tried to shut out the cries as he led Doris and Sims to the jailhouse door. In response to his banging, the door was opened after a moment. As they came down the steps and into the lamplight, he saw Charlie, rifle in hand and his head bandaged.

"Marshal, am I glad to see you!"

Eli motioned Sims and his daughter to the cell, but kept their luggage outside the bars. He checked Sims for guns as they both protested.

"Marshal," the banker said, "you can't do this!"

"You'll be safe in there," Eli assured him.

"They'll tear this place down," Sims protested.

Eli ignored him and turned to Charlie. The man had been

hurt badly and could hardly move as he barred the door again. Then the old man told Eli about Belcher and Elms and how he had had to shoot Elms.

"He say anything?" Eli asked.

"Wasn't time for him to say nothin'. Then the miners came chargin' over. There was a thousand dollars in Elms's pocket. Masters tried to calm them down, but they went wild. They started out lookin' for Sims and ended up burnin' the whole town. Nobody's touched the east side, though."

There was a banging on the door. It was Billy.

"Your mother safe?" Eli asked.

"She went across the bridge to the east side. That's where everyone's gone that got away. But most folks lost everything. There's no stoppin' the fires."

"You see Miss Bennett?" Sims asked.

"No, but she probably went to the east side," Billy said.

Sims was gripping the bars with both hands. "Marshal, at least let me have a gun to defend myself."

"I'm not sure they ain't right about you," Eli said.

"I ain't done nothin' wrong. Because I have a lot of money, they blame me for everything."

"You took a mighty big cut out of everyone's shipment," Charlie reminded him.

"I'm just a normal businessman," Sims claimed.

Eli turned to Billy. "Do me a favor and head Sims's wagon south out of town."

"No!" Sims cried. "All we have left is in there."

"You'd rather they knew you're here?" Eli asked.

"No, but someone could steal it all."

"Clothes can be replaced," Eli told him. "Your skin can't."

As Billy lowered the bar from the door, Sims cried out, "No! Wait! All my gold is in the wagon."

"*Your* gold?" Eli asked.

"That's right. I took only what was mine. You gotta give me what's mine. Just lift up the floor boards and you'll see it. Just bring it here."

Eli shrugged. "All right. Charlie, you and Billy bring in his gold. Then send the wagon out of town."

After the chore was done and the sacks of gold dust and coin were heaped near the desk, Charlie slumped in a chair, exhausted. He said, "Well, I sent the team running south. Can't guarantee they won't be barn sour and come back."

"Eli," Doris pleaded, "do I have to stay in this dirty old cell?"

"You're safer there for now," Eli said, taking up his rifle. "Don't let anyone in but me, Charlie. Billy, you can stay or join your ma."

"I'll stay till you get back," Billy said. "I can shoot a rifle as good as Charlie."

*   *   *

Striding across the clearing, Eli could see that only the hotel still survived, though it was likely to go too. The rest of the town was in ruins or still burning. The mob of miners had dwindled. Horses were running wild in the street. There were no more screams.

Looking to his left across the bridge, he saw crowds of people moving about. The east side had taken them in. It was still a town, after all.

The barber was kneeling by an injured man. A big miner was

carrying two small children toward the east side while their mother trailed behind. The anger had turned into pity for the victims.

Eli supposed that Eve and Gunnison were probably on the east side, but he didn't want to wander far from the jail just now.

He went back there and was let inside.

"Billy," he said, "it looks safe enough. Go on and find your ma. I'll walk with you."

"You gotta stay with us, Marshal," Sims said. "Or let us out. Get us some horses and a pack mule."

Eli ignored the banker and departed with Billy. As they walked across the clearing, the top floor of the hotel roared and collapsed in a heap. They paused to stare at the spectacle, then continued toward the bridge.

"Remember, no one's to know I got Sims in jail."

"Don't worry, Marshal. Look, all the buildings are gone now. They'll have to rebuild everything. I guess folks on the east side will help. Some nice people live over there. They treated me like I was grown up and gave me work."

The flames of the west side cast long shadows in front of Eli and Billy as they walked across the wooden bridge. Billy's mother appeared from the crowd. She was a plump woman in a black shawl, and her face brightened as she clasped Billy in her arms.

"Aw, Ma," he muttered.

"You get over here," she said. "They got hot soup for us. You too, Marshal."

The hot soup was in a great iron kettle over an open fire in front of the dance hall. Coralee, in a bright red gown, was serving and looking worried about the children. The east and west side had mixed and no one seemed to care about the niceties.

Many stood looking back at the flames and ruins, their faces pained with their loss. Others sat huddled together. Some were weeping over lost loved ones.

The miners were subdued and shattered, and some had run away. In front of the Golden Lady, Masters was setting a man's broken leg. Eli started over to him, and then he paused, because the woman helping Masters was Eve Bennett.

She rose when the work was done. Her hair was tied back from her face. She wore a white apron over her green dress.

Turning, she stared at Eli as if she hadn't expected to see him alive. She brightened, and her lips parted with unspoken pleasure. Eli could feel his heart pounding as she approached him.

As they gazed at each other, neither heard the crowd any longer. They saw only each other, here in the night, apart from the world. Her lips trembled as she took a step closer. She looked shattered, broken, but filled with a warmth that was reaching out to him.

Eli ached to draw her into his arms, to protect her. He lifted his hand slowly and touched her face ever so gently. Tears came to her eyes.

Then a rough voice broke the stillness between them. It was a miner demanding attention.

"Marshal, you seen Sims?"

"Why?" Eli asked, hating the interruption.

"He was the cause of all this."

"Did he set the fires?"

"No, I gotta admit we let ourselves go crazy. But at the express office, the safe with our dust was empty. Same at the bank, Marshal. It had to be Sims who took it."

"Or someone with the combination," Eli said.

"He didn't trust nobody," the miner insisted.

"But you have no proof."

"You find Sims and we'll get the proof out of him."

"Maybe he died in the fire."

"We went to his house, but he had packed up and left, him and that girl of his. He's guilty, all right."

"But his leaving isn't proof for the judge."

"Then we'll hang him," the miner growled.

Eli was glad when the man turned away. But Eve was gone now too. He looked for her, but she had disappeared.

He walked around and observed the mingling of east and west. Respectable women gratefully accepted blankets from the dance-hall girls. The saloons were being made into sleeping quarters. The sick and hurt were being cared for, but some lay badly burned and dying.

Eli walked away from the lights of the small fires where people warmed themselves. He stood on the bridge and gazed at what was left of the west side. Now they were all busy with their misery, but he had Sims in jail, and tomorrow would be one big explosion.

TEN

*E*li sat up on his bunk, still weary but unable to sleep. Charlie was coming in the door with a tray of food. The old man's head was still bandaged. He didn't look as if he had slept, either.

As Eli barred the door, Charlie slid some of the food under the cell door for Sims and Doris, then set the tray on the desk. "We gotta share this, Marshal. Didn't want to arouse suspicion by gettin' food for four."

Sims and his daughter were sitting on the cell bunk with blankets around them, sound asleep. Eli let them sleep while he and Charlie ate.

"Town's all gone," Charlie said. "People are walkin' through the ashes, tryin' to find somethin' left. They're still chasin' horses. Lots o' dogs runnin' loose."

"You go ahead and eat, Charlie. I'll find something to eat out there."

"Hope you find somethin' left. Looks like Sherman's march through Georgia."

"Everyone's on the east side mostly."

"Gettin' along too. But when they find out we got Sims, you're gonna need more than me, Marshal. Even the good people out there will wanna hang Sims. They lost everything, and they'll blame him. All your law books won't help you now." Charlie wolfed down his food while Eli checked his six-gun.

"I don't figure you're the same man who rode in here, Marshal. You was just a gunfighter out for a killin'. Next thing you knowed, you was shootin' me out of a tree. Then you went and read them books and talked for me in front of the judge. Maybe you don't even wanna kill this here Tom Cassidy anymore."

"Did you see Gunnison?"

"I saw him goin' into a saloon."

Doris was beginning to stir. Though her father still slept, she stood up and dusted herself off, feeling dirty and weary. She stared at the two men at the desk.

"Eli Cole, you let me out of here."

"No. They'd know your father was here. But tonight, I'll try to get you to the jail in Salerno."

At Eli's mention of the jail, Sims stirred and sat up straight. "You gotta let us out," he said. "We'd never reach Salerno alive."

Eli walked to the door and removed the bar. "Marshal, don't leave us alone with this old coot," Sims pleaded.

"Yeah," Charlie said, "I might do the town a favor and let 'em loose."

"Just don't let anyone in," Eli told him.

Eli left and Charlie barred the door again. "Look, old man," Sims said. "You sneak us out and I'll give you half that gold."

"Half? I got it all right now. You sit back and enjoy your meal, Sims. Be sure and give your daughter enough. Don't be a hog like you been all your life."

"You got no call to talk to me that way," Sims snapped.

"No call? You double-mortgaged me and wiped me out. Why, I even took to sluice-robbin' because of you. I oughta tell the marshal you tried to escape and just blast you right now."

Charlie picked up a shotgun as he sat down. "Just take it easy," Sims muttered.

"Daddy, he's gone crazy."

Sims and Doris backed away to the bunk and shared the food in silence. Charlie cackled and set about finishing his coffee.

There was silence at last in the jailhouse, but out on the street, among the smoking ruins, it wasn't silent. In the quiet of early morning, men and women walked about, searching and weeping. A dog wandered by, sniffing for food.

Eli reached the wooden bridge, where he met Billy.

"Hi, Marshal. Can I go see Charlie?"

"All right, but don't stay long."

"Things are calmed down, Marshal. Them folks, you'd think they'd been friends all their lives. Just 'cause they all lost their money to the same feller."

"Let's hope it lasts."

"Don't think they're gonna listen to any law talk now."

On the east side, there were a lot of people milling about. At the food pot in front of the dance hall, there was a long line. A woman came up to Eli, her puffy face tight with anguish. "I ain't found my man, Marshal. What am I gonna do?"

Eli shook his head, unable to answer.

Another woman came up to him, but she was angry.

"Marshal, you got to find that Sims. He took all we owned. We built up our little shop into a big one, and we trusted him and put everything into his bank. Now it's all gone. You gotta find him and get our money back."

"Yeah," a man from the grub line called. "Find him so we can string 'im up."

Coralee called out from where she was dishing out bacon and beans: "You don't have to stand in line, Marshal."

He waved to her but walked on in the sunlight, watching the faces of the people in line. Men and women, homeless, everything lost, with children playing games at their feet. Many had died in the fires, but he had to deal with the living. It wasn't going to be easy.

A group of miners were in front of the Golden Lady, and he walked toward them. They looked hostile.

"Where's Masters?" Eli asked.

"Inside," one said. "You seen Sims?"

"No, I haven't."

"Well, when we find him, you gotta step aside, Marshal."

"I want to see that fat hide dangling," another man said.

Eli pushed his way through them and entered the crowded saloon. Masters was at the bar. As Eli walked toward him, he looked around and wondered where Eve and Gunnison were.

Masters leaned on the bar as Eli joined him.

"Well, Marshal, you were out of town at the wrong time."

"Seems that way."

"Have a drink."

"No, thanks," Eli said.

"Reckon you know all that happened. The men went a little crazy."

A woman appeared with a cup of steaming coffee for Eli. It tasted good and strong. He looked around the room at the noisy crowd of men from both sides of the bridge, mixing together in a common cause.

"Can you keep 'em in hand now?" Eli asked.

"No promises, Marshal. What's done is done, but as for Sims, he's gonna hang. Not you or any judge is gonna hold this crowd if they find where he's hidin' or where he went."

"There's still a lot you could do to keep a lid on."

"Not likely."

"You know, Masters, when I move on, there's still got to be law in this town. Charlie is too old. There's only one man who could wear this badge. That's you."

Masters shrugged and downed his drink. He turned grim eyes on Eli as he spoke, his voice low: "Well, I reckon, if it was up to me, he'd hang legal- like, after a trial. But I think the trial's been done had, Marshal. Nobody in this town's goin' to stand up for Sims."

Eli finished his coffee and resumed his walk through the crowd. The grub line was shorter now, and he saw Eve Bennett helping Coralee dish out the beans and coffee. But there was still no sign of Will Gunnison.

Eve smiled at him, but she looked distressed. Uneasy, he turned and walked back toward the bridge.

"Wait!" Eve called, hurrying after him.

He paused and looked at her. She was holding a large spoon. An apron was still over her now- tattered dress. She looked weary and confused.

"Are you all right?" he asked.

"Yes, but Will and some other men were out looking for Sims and his daughter. They found their wagon out in the canyon."

"Where are they now?"

"Down the street, forming a posse. They think that Sims and his daughter are somewhere on foot, or that they met someone with horses."

"Is Gunnison riding with this posse?"

"I don't think so."

"Don't tell anyone that you told me about findin' the wagon. I'm not planning to ride with them."

"They don't think they need you," she said, weaving slightly to one side.

"Are you sure you're all right?"

"Yes, I just haven't slept."

"If you need anything, you let me know."

"Yes, I will," she promised, her eyes shining. They gazed at each other a long while in the sunlight, each leaning toward the other. Eli wanted to hold her and never let her go. Yet neither moved a step.

"Eve!" a man called.

They turned to see Gunnison striding along the street toward them. At the same time Masters came out of the saloon and followed Gunnison over to where Eve and Eli were standing.

"Marshal," Gunnison said, glowering, "you're out of line."

Eve was flushed. "Will, I only asked him if they had found any survivors."

Gunnison's thin, swarthy face was dark with jealousy. He looked at Masters, the big leader of the miners, a man he wanted to impress, and he calmed himself.

"Reckon I can be wrong," Gunnison said. "About you and Eve. Come along, honey, you need some rest. You been tendin' these people all night." Masters and Eli stood back and watched as Will marched her away. She turned ever so little and looked back, the way a fawn might when carried away by a predator.

Masters cleared his throat. "Well, now."

"Don't say it," Eli warned.

"All I'm sayin' is that we all know Gunnison is Sims's hired gun. But we can't prove it. Just the same, he may have done some of the killings. If you and he was to fight over his fiance, it would rid us of a big problem."

Eve and Gunnison were disappearing into the crowd. There was pain in his gut, but Eli could do nothing.

Masters said, "I've been thinkin' this whole thing out."

They walked onto the wooden bridge toward the west. Smoking ruins lay ahead. A few people wandered about in the ashes.

"I figure," Masters resumed, "that Sims ain't up in them hills."

"That so?"

"They found his wagon all right, and the bed tore up where he'd hid somethin'. But I figure Sims is right here in town."

"Maybe so."

They reached the clearing, and Masters nodded toward the jail.

"You got that jail all sealed up in the heat. Most other times, you got that door open. I'm figurin' you got Sims and his daughter in there and you're gonna sneak 'em out of town tonight."

Eli met his glance square and didn't flinch.

"Well, sir," Masters said, nodding toward the ruins, "that there mess was partly my doin'. Only one way to set things right. I'm gonna bring a wagon around by the jail around midnight. Me and Charlie can take the old road to Salerno.

Charlie's too old to go it alone. Sims is a fat old fox."

"You'd still be takin' a chance," Eli said.

"Maybe not. You'll have the town's gold. That's all they really want. Oh, sure, if Sims was here, they'd hang him, but the gold's enough. I figure the storekeeper has enough learnin' to go through the books and set the bank right."

Eli studied him in the sunlight. "All right, it's a deal."

"I can't shake your hand, because folks might be watching, but I want you to know I got a lot of respect for you, Marshal, and for that badge. Believe it or not."

"I reckon I always had you figured that way."

Masters grunted and walked back toward the bridge. Eli headed for the jail, wondering how many people besides Masters were figuring Sims had to be here. He noted that his roan had been fed and watered again. He guessed it had to be Charlie's work, because Billy was not around. The animal was half in the shade behind the building. Eli went over to it, and the animal nuzzled him.

Going back to the front, he knocked on the door. After a moment Charlie let him in and reset the bar.

"We gotta get them folks out of here," the old man said. "The longer we wait, the shakier I get. I ain't so sure I want to die for the likes of them." Sims and his daughter were gripping the bars of the cell. They glared at Eli.

"You better get us outta here," Sims whined.

"I might if I heard a little talkin' first," Eli said. He sat down on the edge of his desk and helped himself to some coffee that was left over. "Talking?" Sims snapped. "About what?"

"How you cheated the miners every time you loaned 'em money," Eli said. "And when your express company was shipping their gold, you were robbin' it and getting it back."

"That's a lie! That gold there is all mine. Anything that's missing, they stole before they burned the place. They're all lying."

"Well," Eli said, "I figure Elms and Belcher weren't the only ones you were payin' for information. Now that you can't fork out for anyone, they may come forward."

"Look, Marshal, nothing you can say will make me admit I did anything wrong," the banker said.

"You'd better worry about your hide," Charlie warned him.

Sims stood taller despite his fat body. "Marshal," he growled, "you're wearing the badge. It's your duty to get us out of here alive."

Eli's hawk-like face was dark with thought. There was no way he could get a confession out of this man. There was no proof Sims had had people killed for a box of gold.

"You'll be leaving tonight," Eli said. "Masters and Charlie will take you to Salerno for trial."

"Masters will hang us on the trail."

"He won't, and that makes him a better man than most."

"Eli," Doris said anxiously, "you know I had nothing to do with anything. Please let me out."

"Will you testify?" Eli asked.

"Against my father?" she gasped. She shook her head.

*   *   *

At about midnight there was a knock on the door. It was Billy and Charlie. They came inside and barred the door. Billy handed Eli an envelope.

"From Miss Bennett," Billy said. "It's got some letters and a note writ to Gunnison by Mr. Sims." Eli took them over to the lamp, but he paused to see the dread on Sims's fat face. Biting his lip, Eli opened the large envelope to draw out the papers. They were in Sims's scrawling hand, all right. He had seen it at the bank.

The first letter asked Gunnison and Decker to come to Yellow Creek to "recover" some gold for him and "rid the place" of a few people. There was another note about a job well done but with a warning not to kill any more of the guards. The rest were more of the same, and all were incriminating. "Sims," Eli said, "you're in a heap of trouble."

"This means that you gotta get Gunnison too,"

Billy told Eli. "But he's still out there with the men, searchin' for Sims. All south of here, I think."

"Is Miss Bennett all right?" Eli asked.

"She is right now."

"You go back now, and if you see Gunnison ride into town, you come and tell me. But you tell Miss Bennett not to be speakin' her mind."

"All right, Marshal," the boy said.

"Son," Charlie spoke up, "I see you got a lot of your pa in you."

Proud and beaming, the boy left as Masters entered.

"No moon," Masters said.

Eli showed him the letters, and the big man grinned. "This is what the judge wants. Right, Marshal?"

"Sure is," Eli said. "That's why I'm trustin' it to you and Charlie to carry. You make sure it gets there. I figure to be bringin' Gunnison."

Eli handed Masters a shotgun and rifle. Then he let out Doris and Sims and handed Doris her bag. He stood between Sims and his carpetbag.

"My gold," the banker said.

"That's evidence," Eli snapped.

Masters poked at Sims with the shotgun, shoving him to the door. Doris turned to Eli with a half smile.

"We didn't really get to know each other," she said wistfully.

Eli just shrugged, then watched Masters and Charlie herd them out into the night. Next he closed and barred the door and turned up the lamp. He would need his sleep tonight, because tomorrow he would have to apprehend Gunnison.

He lay back on his bunk and tried to convince himself that he was going after Gunnison for the law. That was the only reason he could accept. He closed his eyes, gun in hand, and wondered how he had strayed so far from his vengeance trail.

ELEVEN

*J*ust before dawn, Eli was awakened by a scratching on the door and what sounded like a whimper. He saw nothing through the peephole, and going to the window, he slid the board aside. He could see the edge of a green dress in the first glow of early light.

Quickly, gun in hand, he went to the door and slid the bar aside. As he opened the door slowly, a crumpled heap rolled against his feet.

Eve lay with her arms bared from the elbows down, and her skin bruised and bleeding. Her hair covered her face. A silent, invisible fist slammed into Eli's gut. He moved around her and checked outside. There was no sign of anyone. He closed and barred the door. Then he knelt, his heart pounding, and lifted her by the shoulders.

As her head rolled back against his arm, he saw the bruises on her cheeks and chin. She opened her eyes for a moment and gazed up at him with tears trickling down her face. Slowly, carefully, feeling her wince with pain, he lifted her into his arms.

Her face was against his chest, and he knew she must hear

the drumming of his heart. She was in pain, and she moaned as he placed her carefully on his bunk. Like a rag doll, she had no visible life even as she looked at him.

Hate was burning in him for the man who had done this to Eve. He brought over the canteen and put it to her lips. After a moment she sipped from it.

"He found out about the letters," she whispered.

"Gunnison did this to you?"

"Yes."

He stood up, fury gripping him.

"Wait," she moaned. "He did it so you'd come out, so he could fight you. He's crazy to get the letters back."

Eli looked down at her. Then he hurried to the door, checking the load of his six-gun.

"Eli, please, no! He's out there waiting."

"Do you figure an ambush?"

"No, but I'm afraid for you."

He put his hand on the bar and looked at her again. He wanted to stay here, to comfort her and wash her face, to hold her. But his anger drove him to pull away the bar.

"Eli! Please!"

But he was out the door and rushing into the early sunlight. He reached the street and squinted toward the bridge. As he pulled his hat down to shade his gaze from the sun, he saw Gunnison on the wooden planks, heading toward him with a crowd at his heels.

Charlie had warned Eli, but here he was, fighting a man whose woman Eli wanted. A dead man's walk. A fool's walk. How fast could his hand be and how clear his brain if he was thinking of Eve? Guilt would slow him down. He would know fear, because he wanted to live. Everything about this was wrong.

He saw Billy crossing over to the jail. He hoped the boy was not going for a weapon. This was no time for anyone but a professional.

The crowd had spread to both sides of the street, and Gunnison was within twenty feet of Eli. Both men stopped to study each other, their hands at their sides.

Eli drew a deep breath. He strained to clear his mind.

"Gunnison," he called, "I'm taking you in. We have evidence against you."

"You got nothing," Gunnison said.

"Drop your gun belt!"

"Marshal, I'm a heck of a lot faster than you."

Eli moistened his dry lips. Another gunfight, but not of his choosing. He hated this man's guts. Who was the faster gun, he didn't know, but with the badge on his chest, he had to try to arrest the man first. It was the hardest job he had ever attempted.

"You're scared!" Gunnison roared. "Cold yeller!"

The crowd moved away from the line of fire. The sun was higher now. Sweat was on Eli's face. And for the first time in a fight, on his hands too.

Ten years of killing without a second thought, and now there was sweat on his hands. Guilt was hot in his belly. All because he knew that if Gunnison died, Eve would be free.

"Look at 'im!" Gunnison shouted. "He's hidin' behind that badge."

"You're under arrest," Eli said.

"No way I can be arrested by a dead man." Gunnison laughed.

"Sims is on his way to another jail," Eli said. "He'll see you hang right along with him."

"You have to get me there first."

The two men faced each other in a long silence. Eli became aware of his pulse pounding in his ears. His throat was parched.

Meanwhile, Billy was bringing Eve from the jail. Tough men turned and cringed at the sight of her. She stumbled and fell some twenty feet from the crowd. She tried to rise but fell on her elbow. Mrs. Whitaker came over and tried to hold her up in her arms. Billy knelt and whispered to his mother, "The marshal won't draw. He won't fight because he's in love with her."

Eve opened her eyes. She drew Billy to her and whispered something that startled him. The boy stood up and turned toward the gunmen.

Gunnison was prancing about for the crowd. "You saw me take Decker, Marshal," he shouted.

"You think you can take me? You ain't gettin' this gun unless you do."

Eli felt sweat running down his back. His shirt was soaked. He couldn't move.

"Shall I turn my back, Marshal? Give you a better chance?"

Eli's throat had a knot somewhere deep inside. He didn't answer. There was turmoil within him.

"Come on, Marshal, or are you yellow clean through? Where's this brave Eli Cole we been hearin' about?"

Again there was a silence. And Billy moved closer.

"All right," Gunnison said. "If you won't draw, I will. See this silver dollar? When it hits the dust, I'm going to blast you."

Eli froze. The crowd was hushed. Gunnison tossed the silver dollar high in the air. It glittered in the sun.

"Marshal!" Billy cried. "He's Tom Cassidy!"

Eli saw the truth in the man's startled fury.

As the dollar hit the dust, both men drew. Eli's rage lifted his revolver in the fastest draw he had ever made. Shots rang out, their echoes bouncing in the breathless silence.

Hit hard in the chest, Eli staggered back from the blow. Blood splattered his shirt near his side. Instinctively, he drew back the hammer on his Colt, ready to fire again. The weapon wavered in his grasp.

Before Eli died, he had to kill this man, this animal. This was Cassidy, the last and worst of the hunted.

Slowly, his enemy was lowering his revolver.

Cassidy had no color in his face. His hand was on his throat, blood trickling through his fingers.

"Eli Cole," he gasped "For ten years—"

Eyes wild, Cassidy choked on his blood, and the wreck of a man dropped to his knees. He looked drained of life, yet he didn't fall.

Eli was drained as well, but of vengeance. It was over. He felt no relief, no satisfaction. Just a dead emptiness.

Eyes glassy, Cassidy fired into the dirt twice. The shots echoed in the stillness.

His gun still in his hand, Eli staggered over to look down at Cassidy. Pain was shooting through Eli's side, and blood trickled down his shirt. Yet he refused to think about his own death, not until Cassidy was gone.

Cassidy moaned and closed his eyes. Then he fell forward flat on his face, dead.

Billy ran to Eli's side and grabbed him as he swayed. The boy struggled to hold him erect.

"Miss Bennett found out he was Cassidy a long time ago," Billy said. "But she wasn't gonna tell you. Not till she realized you wasn't goin' to draw."

Eli fell to one knee, and Billy tried to hold him, but Eli went down on his back, clasping his chest. The barber was bending over him as blackness shut out the world.

Eli saw nothing but whirling night. He felt pain, but he was more aware of an emptiness. Cassidy was dead now. They were all dead. Yet nothing could change what had happened to his family. Heartsick in his delirium, he welcomed the black pool in which he lay.

Then, strangely, he felt as if he were being transported to a place cold and distant, as if his soul were leaving his body. He could see himself bending over Eve and touching her face. She was weeping for him. Desperately, he tried to reach her. He wasn't ready to die.

Suddenly, he was whirling back into that pool of darkness. Pain racked his body again. He heard noise but saw nothing.

Then there was a tiny light—a lamp. A face was looking down at him. The face was square and somber. It was Marshal Kline, and they were in a bedroom with red curtains.

Eli realized that he was still alive. He tried to lift his hands, to touch something and make sure. But pain stopped him.

"Well, it's about time," Kline said. "You've been out for nearly three days."

Eli swallowed hard, trying to grasp the situation.

"You lost a heap of blood," Kline added. "They had to dig deep for that slug. But you'll make it."

Eli tried to speak, but no sound passed his lips.

"You done me proud," Kline told him. "When you're better,

we'll have us a talk. Then we'll be goin' to Salerno for the trial. Hear you're mighty good in the courtroom."

Eli wanted to say he was headed for Oregon, that he'd had enough. But the words didn't come.

"Another thing," Kline said. "We got a lady here who's been awake two whole days tendin' you. She finally fell asleep an hour ago. Want me to wake her?"

Eli tried to rise, and Kline helped him turn slightly.

Eve was slumped in a chair by the window, with sunlight on her hair. She wore a blue dress. Her face was still discolored from the blows, but she had never looked more beautiful to him.

Eli watched as Kline shook her gently. She sat up and rubbed her eyes. When she saw Eli, the most lovely smile in the world came to her face.

Kline helped her to her feet, and she leaned on him as she was guided to a chair by the bed. She reached out for Eli and took his cold hand in both of hers. Her touch warmed him to his toes.

He saw the new freedom in her face. Her father was safe from whatever lies or truth could have him hanged. She was free of Cassidy. Suddenly, Eli was afraid that she would run away.

"Reckon I'll just come back later," Kline said.

They didn't hear him leave. Eve rose from her chair and bent forward. Her lips were velvet on Eli's. It was as if a miraculous tonic were flooding his veins.

They couldn't speak. Their love was too new and sensitive.

Eli Cole had reached the end of his vengeance trail. Never again would he be alone. Eve slumped back in her chair and smiled at him with wonder in her eyes.

He looked from her to the badge that Kline had pinned on

his fresh, clean shirt. Somehow he knew that they would never get to Oregon. Kline would see to that. But Eli didn't care.

Eli Cole had come home.

ABOUT THE AUTHOR

*W*estern novelist and screenwriter **Lee Martin** grew up on cattle ranches in Northern California. Martin began writing in the third grade and, later in life, sold 43 short stories, before turning to novels with 23 now published. Martin is a prolific writer of screenplays, mostly Westerns.

Martin's screenplay for *Shadow on the Mesa*, starring Kevin Sorbo, Wes Brown, and Gail O'Grady, was based on Martin's novel of the same title (Five Star Publishing, 2014). The movie was the second-highest-rated and second-most-watched original movie in Hallmark Movie Channel's history when it premiered in 2013. The film also won the prestigious Wrangler Award given by the National Cowboy & Heritage Museum in Oklahoma City for Best Original TV Western Movie.

Martin's recent novels, *The Grant Conspiracy*, *The Last Wild Ride*, and *Fury at Cross Creek*, received rave reviews from *True West Magazine* and were based on Martin's screenplays, as is *Fast Ride to Boot Hill*. *In Mysterious Ways*, Martin's new modern suspense Western, received great reviews from *Kirkus Reviews* and *Midwest Book Reviews*.

Martin recently left the practice of law to write full-time, concentrating on Western screenplays and novels, often converting one to the other. Several of Martin's screenplays are under option by producers. To learn more, visit Lee Martin Westerns on Facebook.

www.ingramcontent.com/pod-product-compliance
Lightning Source LLC
Chambersburg PA
CBHW031237260626
47169CB00007B/2347